The Weeping Triangle

Taniform Martin Wanki

Langaa Research & Publishing CIG
Mankon, Bamenda

Publisher
Langaa RPCIG
Langaa Research & Publishing Common Initiative Group
P.O. Box 902 Mankon
Bamenda
North West Region
Cameroon
Langaagrp@gmail.com
www.langaa-rpcig.net

Distributed in and outside N. America by African Books Collective
orders@africanbookscollective.com
www.africanbookcollective.com

ISBN: 9956-726-06-0

© Taniform Martin Wanki 2011

1

'The second time brandished as the world's most corrupt country in a row and almost on its way to becoming first again for the third time.' Those thoughts kept tormenting me as I sat in that taxi heading to the ministry of education that Tuesday morning of Febuary 25th. I remembered my numerous friends around the world and what they could have been thinking of me and my country with its newly acquired status. Then the words of Simon Woods, a British friend who lived in London, re-echoed in my mind.

"It seems corruption is what people of your country know best. I think it could be a good commodity to export to other countries. Please tell your government that if they are interested in selling it to the outside world, I could help to advertise it, perhaps on the London Stock Exchange," he told me in a phone conversation I had with him two days earlier.

Though he was just trying to crack a joke as usual, my pride was hurt and I was ashamed of what was happening to my country.

"This is what happens when someone stays in power too long. New ideas seem to elude them and they still feel they are indispensable in the life of the nation," I said unconsciously to the hearing of the driver.

"Son, I do understand fully well what you are talking about," he said to me though I was not really talking to him. "That is why things are better in countries where there are changes at the helm every four or five years than those where constitutions are there to serve only the interest of those in power. I have never understood why an individual would imagine that he is the only one endowed with the wisdom and experience to govern. Does thinking like that mean that he is going to remain there forever? Of course not... when his time is up, he is going to go and should not think that the country would cease to exist after him. Corruption is the product of a failed system resulting from bad governance. You can talk to the authorities who would admit that corruption is a problem but they would be quick to defend themselves by saying that corruption is a worldwide phenomenon as if being a worldwide phenomenon should make it legitimate. Anyway, we are already old and cannot do anything about this present situation but are counting on young people like you to turn things around for our children."

There was a lot of emotion in his voice as he spoke. I did not need the services of an expert to tell me that Harley Simon, the driver, as I could read on his identification taxi badge, was equally tired of the situation. He was definitely boiling with anger as were many other people whose hopes of a blissful life faded away with the passing days. He remained pensive, shook his head, sighed several times and then opened his mouth. But no words emerged. I would have engaged him in a discussion which I thought could enable us to pour out our grievances to each other as I sat just next to him. But I didn't for fear that I might have broken his concentration or even worse, caused him to crash the car. I sat still and silent, thinking of what I might encounter at the ministry. Then after a while some words finally fell from his lips.

"Only heaven will judge these people who have decided to enjoy themselves by making life a living hell for us the common people. They have devised a strategy which seems to be a motto and it is 'let the underprivileged, poor and unemployed die so that those in power can survive," he said in desperate resignation.

The anguish and anger that had built up for long made him a ticking time-bomb and I did not know which words of hope I could tell him to ease his pain. His sad words and desperation seemed to have chased all ideas from my head leaving it completely empty. Perhaps it was because I could feel his desperation since we all belonged to the common class of strugglers. Out on the street, people were hurrying to their different destinations, some on foot and others on commercial motor-bikes. Young girls of school going age carried trays of fruits on their heads moving around selling. Their male counterparts pushed trucks or wheel-barrows craning their eyes left and right in the hopes of having someone employ them to transport a few items from one place to another in exchange for a few coins. The sun was shining brightly that morning but its rays it seemed could only illuminate the city and pierce hard into people's flesh but could not dispel the darkness and uncertain future that hung over people's heads.

It was 08:45 and the taxi had just come to a halt. We had arrived at a round-about and were waiting for the traffic light to turn green. A white Toyota Starlet sped past us without stopping with a young boy of about sixteen at the steering wheel.

"What could be chasing that young man or what is he running after?" another passenger who sat directly behind me asked. At that moment, it was difficult to tell.

3

"You are running to your grave," Simon shouted after him though he was already too far to have heard what he said. Everyone in the taxi sighed.

"If you ask that young man for his driving license, he would produce a valid one though the law in this country says youths below eighteen are not allowed to drive," Simon went on. "Do you know what kills most people in this country? It is not HIV/AIDS, malaria, road accidents or cancer. It is bribery and corruption. With money, one can produce or buy anything in this country." Everybody sighed again.

The light soon turned green and we were on the move again, only this time the only noise was that made by the engine. Some 600 meters from the round-about, we met a crowd of people who surrounded a stationary truck loaded with logs of timber. Under the truck was a white Toyota Starlet or should I say 'the wreckage of a white Toyota Starlet'. We recognized it as the one that sped past us without stopping at the round-about. Traffic slowed down considerably at that point and we were able to see how the boy was extracted from the Starlet and put into another taxi to be taken to the hospital. Blood was oozing out of his nose and forehead. My blood ran cold as I saw what happened to the young man.

"Do you see what I was telling you?" Simon asked. "That is the prize for trading our consciences for money and for breaking rules that we ourselves have laid down. I only hope he survives."

I did not make any comments as I didn't want to see only bribery and corruption as the probable cause of the accident. What if the parents or guardians or relative of the boy left the car at home and he got it out without their knowledge? Boys at that age can be very mischievous and adventurous. One could not predict what they could be up to the next minute.

It was 09:15 when the taxi stopped in front of the Ministry of Secondary Education and I alighted. It was a gigantic and magnificent eight floor storey building which was built in the form of the letter C. It was fenced all round and there were heavily armed men in uniform guarding the main and other entrances into the building. Only those who worked in the building or anyone dressed in an expensive European three piece suit were allowed in at that time of the day. I just wore a simple T-shirt and a pair of trousers and could not enter. The reason given for not letting people in at that moment was that the minister was still in his office situated on the eighth floor of the building and was to leave at 11:00. It was only after his departure that anybody was allowed to go into the building. That was how things were every working day at the ministry. I therefore had to wait until the minister left at 11:00.

For the next one hour forty five minutes that I had to wait, I spent the time observing the people and the activities they carried out around the ministry. A good number of them, especially women, sold cooked food while others and some as young as thirteen sold items ranging from books, newspapers, fruits, right down to kitchen utensils. From time to time, workers from inside the ministry came out to have something to eat. Some of them sat out there for more than an hour conversing with food vendors even long after they had finished eating. I began to ask myself if all that waste of time was because there was no work for them or if there was no one to attend to. It seemed that having one's name on the state's payroll was more important than actually working for the state whole heartedly. That kind of behaviour was a clear indication that someone at the top was not doing his or her job.

At exactly 10:50, the main gate into the ministry building was flanged open and a chain of latest four wheel drive Toyota Prados drove out of the ministry premises. It was the minister leaving. As all the vehicles were the same colour, it was difficult to say which one the minister was in. After his departure, everyone could go into the ministry building unrestricted.

I got into the building and decided that I would use the lifter to get to the seventh floor where room 404 was situated (located?). It was in that room that all advancement issues were handled. There were three lifters and the last time I got to the ministry anyone could use any of them. But on that day, I saw something different. On the door of the second lifter was a written sign that said 'For Workers Only' and the third door said, 'For the Minister Only'. So, only the first one was meant for the public and from all indications, it was out of use because of some mechanical problems. What really intrigued me was not what was written on the doors of the second and third lifters but it was the presence of some men in uniform well armed around there. Perhaps they were there to make sure no one broke the rules. I read no sense in all of that and definitely was not in the mood to start asking questions which would have only led to quarrels. I settled on the last option which was to take the stairs.

The stairs were really crowded as many people used them. It took me ten minutes to get to the seventh floor and I immediately moved into room 404 and shut the door behind me. There was a woman sitting behind a table looking seemingly happy. There were some two other tables to show that there were three of them working in that office. But, the other two workers were not present while I was there.

"Welcome and have a seat. I know those stairs are not easy to climb," she said smiling.

Her smile gave me a sense of confidence and zeal to think that I could talk with her without any fear.

"Thank you," I appreciated.

"What can I do for you?" she asked still smiling.

"I came all the way from Bamenda town to see if I could hand in documents for my advancement. I just thought that after putting in eight years, I was entitled to it," I told her.

"I think everyone who is hard working should be rewarded accordingly," she said. "Can I have your documents?"

I opened my file and took out my documents which I handed to her. While she was flipping through them I asked her why men in uniform did not need to leave the provinces to bring documents to the capital city for their advancements to be effected as those of us in the teaching core did.

"You do not carry guns and so no one is afraid of you," she told me jokingly. I felt hurt by her comments. I did not know why. I knew the system perfectly well and how it functioned. Perhaps I felt hurt because I did not want anyone reminding me of the dirty system I lived in or maybe it was because teachers and men in uniform were all public sector workers and that disparity was not supposed to exist. But one thing was certain and it was the fact that her comments were open to many interpretations. After thanking her for receiving me so warmly and accepting my documents, I rose to leave but she stopped me.

"Why are you just leaving like that?" she asked

"What do you mean? I've given you my documents and you've confirmed that they are all intact. Is there something else I have to do?" I asked with a lot of curiosity.

"Yes of course, you have to sprinkle oil on your documents," she replied smiling.

"Sprinkle oil? And what kind of oil are we talking about here? Oil, no matter which one you are referring to would destroy my documents, don't you think so?" I asked.

My last question changed the expression on her face and the smile on her lips dried up. She sat still for a while and tried to regain her composure after my question made her tense.

"Why do I have the impression that you are not a citizen of this country? What I'm asking is for you to leave something to motivate the person who would handle your file," she explained.

"Please Madam, do not feel offended. But is the person to handle my file not employed by the state and paid to do just that?" I asked.

There was dead silence. She just sat there staring at me.

"So you mean to tell me that without any motivation from me my file would be neglected? By the way, how much are we talking about here?" I asked teasingly.

Her face lit up again but she never had the time to tell me the amount because another person who must have been waiting outside for a long time got tired and decided to force his way in. The man must have been in his mid 50s. The woman tried in vain to plead with him to wait outside for a few more minutes. Sensing that pleading was not going to work, she resorted to threats and insults. Those too did not work. The man was bent and that made me happy. In the midst of that chaos I wished her a wonderful day and walked out. I had to squeeze my way through a crowd that was waiting outside Room 404 to be attended to. Taking into consideration the amount of time I spent in the office just to submit my documents, it was possible that about half of those outside the office would not be attended to. The only thing those outside could do to speed up the process was to slot 2000 FRS notes into the files they had to submit. That way the receiver of the files would quickly check the documents submitted and would politely tell the owner those that were incorrect if there were any. On the other hand if there was no money accompanying the files to be submitted, they were still collected but they were going to end up in drawers unattended to until the motivation fee was paid. Whenever the owner came to check the progress of his or her file, he or she was asked to 'go and come tomorrow'. That phrase was always used to get even those who were stubborn and claimed to be incorruptible to comply. Those who never understood what 'go and come tomorrow' meant paraded the corridors of the offices for days, weeks, months and even years. They were always given flimsy excuses before being asked to 'go and come tomorrow'.

Another strategy to get owners of files that needed some processing to pay the illegal motivation fee was to collect the documents and then keep telling them each time they came to check on the progress of their files that the boss had not been able to sign them for one reason or another. Once the desperate owners paid the motivation fee, their files moved one step or two and the process started all over again. Those who never understood the language remained at the same spot. That explained why there had been numerous reports of files that had gone missing in the ministry of education or the public service.

'Was that going to be the fate of my file since I did not comply?' I wondered as I started descending the stairs again. But then, if asking for motivation was the order of the day, why was the presence of the other person so much of a problem? Did it matter if he was there? Those questions and others kept tormenting me as I walked down the stairs of the ministry building. I then remembered a good number of colleagues who had worked for years without any promotion or advancement. I remembered particularly Mr. Fru William and Mr. Penn Samuel who both worked for 25 years without any advancement. Mrs. Lean Debora worked for 35 years and only received her advancement thanks to the assistance of John Shu, another colleague who understood the game and played it well. He became acquainted with all those in charge of handling the advancement files of all public sector workers in the ministry. When the accrued arias of Mrs. Lean Debora finally came out, she had to surrender 35 percent of the money to Mr. John Shu for his services. Though she was not happy surrendering such a high percentage of what she had laboured for all her life, she was still contented with the balance she had. With time many civil servants who became frustrated with the long years of work with no advancements started soliciting the help of Mr. John Shu. That made him become very rich from the high percentages he charged his clients. His wealth soon attracted others who decided to join the trade. I could remember Mr. Tom Wayne who abandoned his students in Government High School Njinteh, to become a professional file chaser in the ministry. He got one of his friends who taught in a private school just nearby to handle some of his classes while he was away. He promised his friend one quarter of his salary every month but they sometimes had problems over payments. Unfortunately, Mr.

John Shu died some eleven months ago under some very mysterious circumstances and Tom Wayne, two months later. Many people attributed their deaths to the money their clients had to give them grudgingly. Others called it retributive justice. Whether that was true or not was not very important to me. Many colleagues complained of their numerous files which were still in their keeping. Some succeeded in retrieving theirs through the intervention of their widows while the unlucky ones had to start compiling new documents and begin the whole process afresh. What a nightmare!!!

The government made an announcement shortly before Tom Wayne died which temporarily put smiles on people's faces. It announced that from then on the advancement documents of public sector workers were going to be channelled through the different regional delegations instead of the owners abandoning work to travel to the capital city to chase files. Many people welcomed that development because it put out the unscrupulous middlemen. That was just an announcement coming from a government which in terms of promises had a very bad track record. I received the announcement with some scepticism given that presidential and parliamentary elections were just around the corner. I was pretty certain that the government was just canvassing for votes with such an announcement and my fears were justified. The regional delegations were flooded with advancement documents. Some of them were forwarded and eventually processed. The government used the few that were treated to reiterate its commitment to always make life better for its citizens. That presented another opportunity to promise better days ahead if the ruling party was voted back in office. The middlemen sunk into recession as their services were no longer solicited. But in my country where there was a big difference between making promises and effecting promises, the so much heralded government's good intentions suffered a setback. Most of the advancement documents ended up in the delegations without any processing which soon brought the middlemen back into business. It was as a result of the government's failure to keep its promise that I found myself in the capital city handling my advancement documents in person after resolving not to employ the services of the middlemen. "How long would the vast majority of public sector workers be allowed to prey on by shylock middlemen?" remained a lingering question whose answer was blowing in the wind.

2

I had planned to travel back to Bamenda Town immediately I handed in my advancement documents. But with what happened at Room 404, I decided to give my plans a second thought. I decided to cancel my trip and to spend another night in the capital, to return to Room 404 the next morning and find out what became of my file after I left.

I decided not to board a taxi as I got out of the ministry premises. I preferred to walk a few miles before boarding one. I wanted to use the opportunity to feed my eyes on the magnificent buildings and monuments around central town. One striking thing I discovered was the number of garbage heaps. They looked more or less like small mountains. Anybody who was in central town could use them to give directives to someone who could not find his or her way. The sad thing about it all was that the garbage was dumped just by the road sides and some even extended to the road, contributing to the heavy traffic congestion. But each financial year huge funds were allocated for the collection and treatment of urban waste in all the towns and cities of the country. Whatever happened to such funds remained a mystery. I did not want to develop a headache on the issue.

I had walked about two miles when I found myself in front of a ten storey building. It was very close to the road and the frontage was covered with gravel. The walls were covered with Italian ceramic tiles which made it very beautiful at least from the outside. In front was a sign board with the inscription 'Welcome to Hotel Des Amours'. A young girl of about 18 jumped out of the hotel like a frog out of hot water and ran as fast as her legs could carry her. She wore only a

13

mini skirt, a breast wear and was bear footed. She covered a distance of about 100 meters, stopped and boarded the first available taxi that came her way. It was crystal clear that she was running for her dear life and I did not think that the direction she was running to was as important as her safety. But as curious as all the other people around there, I waited to see what was after the young lady. It was a woman who must have been in her early or mid 40s that emerged from the hotel sweating and panting less than three minutes after the young lady ran out. From all indications they must had been using the stairs probably from the 7th floor. She enquired from one of the bystanders the direction taken by the young girl who just ran out. One of them indicated it to her by the show of hand. She headed towards the indicated direction but soon had to turn back as she could not find any trace of her 'enemy.'

"That young prostitute and husband snatcher will hear from me today," she said to the hearing of everyone as she approached the hotel premises.

Just then a man almost in his mid 50s jumped out of the main door of the hotel as well. He wore a blue shirt which was not well buttoned and held his tie and suit in his hand. He hurriedly moved to a Toyota Land Cruiser which was parked in front of the hotel, kicked it and drove off as fast as he could without taking his wife. She boarded a taxi which headed towards the same direction as the man.

"These sugar daddies and young girls, we shall continue to hear of them for a long time to come," said one bystander who stood near me.

"There are mostly these rich men who do these things," said another.

"Men, rich or poor, they are not to be trusted…. They are all dogs", said yet another. Since most of the bystanders were women and all their comments were aimed at castigating men, I did not want to start an argument there by trying to stage some sort of defence. I'm sure they would have fallen on me like bees. I hurriedly left the place just to keep the temptation at bay though I did not like the way they generalized things.

I decided to board a taxi to Bonas, a student residential area which people fondly refer to as Sodom and Gomorra where I spent the previous night in the house of Jacob, a university mate. I got there at 14:52 and Jacob was already back from work. He was a typist at the university secretariat. He asked me if I had already booked for the 22:00 trip and I told him that my plans had changed. I recounted all what happened at the ministry that morning and equally of my decision to go back there the next day. He pitied me and many other public workers who found themselves in the same situation. But there was nothing he could do.

I wanted to make maximum use of the time I still had ahead of me and so told Jacob that I intended visiting a friend, Njom Mathew at Ntuba, an area situated some 30 km in the outskirts of the nation's capital. Jacob had no objection since I promised returning that same day. I left the house and got to the highway in no time and immediately found a mini bus heading to Ntuba. I got in and filled the only empty seat that was left in the bus. In all, we were thirteen in a bus originally meant to carry a maximum of nine persons. It was very uncomfortable and people didn't speak as we went along. There was music in the bus but it was almost over shadowed by the noise made by the engine which was already too old. Though the road was well tarred, smoke filled the bus each time we ascended a slope no matter how small it was. Ascending was a real task in itself given the very old nature of the engine. There were moments when the bus had real difficulties ascending that some of the passengers had to alight and cover a short distance on foot so that the bus could be lighter to get up a little slope. At other times smoke filled the bus to an extent that some passengers started coughing. At times the bus had to stop completely and the passengers would alight so that the smoke dissipated before they got back in. Each time the passengers complained, the driver would jokingly say that the smoke helped to kill mosquitoes in the bus. His comments made some people laugh and others annoyed. The numerous check points on the way did not help matters. Lucky enough everyone in the bus had his or her ID card. From time to time the driver would place a 500 Frs. bank note in his car documents before handing them to the police officer. That was the game and they who plied the road understood it.

About some three kilometres from Ntuba, I heard my stomach rumble. I had eaten some beans and a loaf of bread I bought from a hawker outside the ministry that day. I stayed put hoping that I could ignore it until I got to Ntuba. That was not to be. The rumbling intensified to the extent that my neighbour asked me if I was alright. I said yes though I knew things were not ok. A cold wave ran down my body from head to toe. I felt it more in my legs as they sort of got heavy. That was an indication that something nasty was building up within me. I immediately asked the driver to stop the car. He tried to ask why I wanted him to stop without looking at me. I did not respond. I just sat still and soon felt sweat running down my spine. The driver then turned round to ask me again why I wanted him to stop. The expression on my face was enough to tell him that something was terribly wrong. He stopped by the side of the road and I jumped out. I asked him not to wait for me. He took off immediately I said that. I needed to cover about 25 meters to get out of sight into a farm. That distance looked like a kilometre. The mess in me dictated the pace at which I had to move. When I tried to run, it threatened to come out and I had to slow down. At last I made it to an area in the farm that looked like a perfect hideout. Even someone who strayed into the farm intentionally or accidentally could not easily spot me. I had just enough time to dig a small hole in which I deposited the mess. What was annoying was that it didn't come out quietly. It was accompanied by some intermittent noises. If someone had walked into the farm at that moment, such noises would have betrayed my presence. And really it almost happened as immediately I had finished depositing the mess, a man and a woman ran into the farm and went much further from where I was. They looked very excited as they were all smiles. I decided not to let my curiosity get the better of me. I just sat a few meters from where I deposited the mess to enjoy a little breeze which started blowing. The sweat which kept forcing itself out of my pores when I was under stress started drying off with the passing breeze. It felt really good and I wished it could last longer but I had to go.

I got back to the high way and soon saw a commercial bike rider who was looking for passengers. I stopped him and just as I stood there negotiating how much I had to pay him for the remaining distance that still separated me from my friend's house, many other bikes by-passed us with three young men or more on a single bike. What was shocking was the break neck speed at which they were going. It was difficult to tell what they were all racing after. Immediately I concluded my negotiation with the taxi bike rider, I warned him not to speed. He accepted but on the way I had to tap him on the shoulder every now and then to ask him to slow down. It seemed the love for speed was inborn in them and they got into it sometimes unconsciously. That love for speed could not go without setbacks. Most accident wards in major hospitals in the country had been given names of different motor-cycle marks because of the numerous victims they made on the highway each day. It seemed the commercial bike riders had their brakes not on the bikes they rode on but on the back bumpers of people's cars. I sometimes had the impression that they often forgot that their machines had brakes. I had no intention of ending up in any of the 'Lifang , Nanfang or Okada ward' in any hospital and therefore had to keep the motor-bike rider under control.

I got to Mathew's house in no time. It was a simple two rooms and a parlour. I knocked on the door which was well locked and there was no response. I no longer had the phone number he gave me because I deleted it after dialling once, and was informed by the network operator that the number no longer existed in their network. I thought of going back but soon heard the door making noises. It was Mathew in person and he fell on me with open arms as he came out. We wasted no time outside as he pressured me to get into the house very fast. I did not resist and asked no questions. Once we were inside the house, he locked the door again and made sure it was well locked. I was very uncomfortable with what I saw him doing and asked him why he had to lock the door when there was still daylight. He responded that 'Condom City' where he lived was very dangerous after 17:30 and he did not want to take any chances. He opened the door curtain and peeped outside as he spoke. That was not convincing

18

enough to me and I insisted on knowing what was going on. He did not want to explain anything but instead asked me to go in and have a rest promising at the same time that we would talk later. I started suspecting that my friend might have been in some sort of trouble and was using his house as a hideout. My fears were to be confirmed less than 15 minutes after I entered the house. Some persistent knocks could be heard on the door. I supposed that there were two people knocking at the same time. Mathew stayed put and pleaded with me not to make any noise by gesturing. I did as he said but the silence was not enough to make those who were outside knocking give up.

I soon became uncomfortable with the insecurity and uncertainty that was building around there. I could not imagine that I left the capital city because I had a friend at heart, only to be wrapped up in something I knew nothing about at his residence. In fury, I asked him to open the door or I was going to do it myself. He did and a man who must have been in his mid 50s walked in alongside some two uniform officers. The one who was higher in rank ordered Mathew to come out and follow them to the police station. He asked them if they had a warrant for arrest and they threatened to beat him up mercilessly if he asked another stupid question. Mathew was not the kind of character who would give in to threats. He told them that he was not going anywhere and added that he was a law student and knew all his rights. That comment was enough to scare them. Men in uniform had some category of people they were afraid of and they were teachers and lawyers. They usually argued with and got humiliated by teachers and were always threatened by lawyers. But they dreaded lawyers most since they did not know the law which a good number of them claimed to

19

represent and found themselves in uniform more because formal education was too problematic for them. As a result, university law students by virtue of their language power and their ability to quote some sections of the law whether true or false always succeeded in instilling a great amount of fear in them. That was a good method to curb their rate of brutality and intimidation for which they were notorious. Mathew understood that very well and said he wanted to deal only with the state council. The senior uniform officer understood that he was dealing with someone who did law and opted for a diplomatic solution to the problem that brought them there. He asked the man who brought them to Mathew's house to sort things out amicably. The man accepted and they all sat down on the chairs in the sitting room. The senior uniform officer asked Mathew if he sold a phone to the man two days before and Mathew admitted doing so. In his next question, the officer sought to know if the phone was working before it was sold to the man. Mathew responded that it was working and also added that the man used it to make a call right in front of him. The man confirmed what Mathew said but insisted that Mathew was dishonest as he knew that the phone was not functioning properly. The senior police officer then asked Mathew what prompted him to sell his mobile phone.

"Two days ago, I was really hard up financially and desperately needed 10.000frs. I went to Ntuba village Square and waited for any Good Samaritan to come along and he came. He sat near me at Pleasure Bar and while he was drinking I decided to talk to him about my problem. I told him I badly needed 10,000frs to solve a problem which was on my throat. Coincidentally, he needed a phone and I was prepared to part with mine for any amount so long as it was not less than 10.000 Frs. He proposed 9000 Frs. but I told him that 9999 Frs. could not solve my problem. So, he gave me the 10.000 Frs. I badly needed it and I hurried off to solve my problem. He used the phone to make a call in front of me before I left and I don't know why he has brought you here now," he explained.

"Ok, he has discovered that the phone is not working and he has decided to bring it back for you to refund his money," the senior uniform officer said.

"If he wants me to take my phone back, it should be working the way it was when I gave it to him," Mathew responded.

That last statement angered the man and he wanted Mathew to be picked up and taken to the police station without any further delay. But I think there was fear on the part of Mathew and the uniform officers. Mathew's claim of knowing the law and wanting to deal directly with the state council was already a hindrance to the men in uniform as they could not apply force, added to the fact that they had no arrest warrant. Mathew on his part was just playing tough and I think he knew very well that if he was taken to the police station, he would have had serious problems. So, after so many threats and counter threats Mathew agreed to take back his phone and refund the old man's money but not without giving conditions.

"I have an aunt who sends me 5000 francs as pocket allowance every month. Out of that 5000 francs, I'll be giving him 200 francs which means that in a year I will pay him 1200 francs," Mathew explained.

"What!!!" exclaimed the man. "I thought you were going to talk about 1000 francs or at least 500 francs every month but you are talking of 200 francs. That is an insult.

The senior uniform officer calmed the man down who had already bent the sleeves of his shirt in preparation for a fight. He then turned to Mathew and asked him to be more reasonable. Mathew told him that he could not accept to pay more than 200 francs because if he did, he would probably starve by the end of the next month. So, the senior uniform officer sought to know when Mathew thought he could pay all the money.

"We are in 2007… let's just say 2016 or 2017 to be really sure," he said.

The man got really frustrated with such remarks, grabbed the dead phone and dashed it against the wall which shattered into pieces.

"Let's say that the 10.000 francs I gave you was a form of help," the man said and got out of Mathew's house. The uniform officers followed him with the junior one laughing. Mathew breathed a sigh of relieve when they finally got out of sight.

I did not allow him to have a seat or ask me any question as I immediately confronted him on what I just saw. He admitted that his phone was bad before he sold it to the man. I had some really harsh words for him. I told him that he was lucky that those men in uniform were not smart enough. They would have started by drawing their conclusions on the fact that he locked his door and did not open immediately they knocked. That was evidence enough that he knew what he did was wrong. I asked him what country he wanted those 'old people', as he referred to those in power, to hand over to when young people like him that the nation needed badly had such dubious character. He defended himself by saying that times were hard and he had to use his head to survive. Though I agreed with him that times were hard, I still retorted that duping someone in the name of survival was not the best option. I asked him if the money he dubiously took from the man had not finished and he said that there was no franc left. I felt so disgusted and did not want to talk about it anymore. I told him that I just decided to come over with no intention of spending the night though my initial intention was to do so. I just thought that I had to be careful. I could not tell what could come next if I decided to spend the night with Mathew. Besides, trouble could not discriminate between innocent and guilty people and I had no intention of paying for any crime which must have been committed by my friend. We chatted for a short while and I left again for the capital city.

3

I got to Jacob's house at about 19:30 and he asked me how things went. I told him that everything went well just to prevent him asking further questions. I did not tell him of the scene at Mathew's house. I just went to the bathroom and had a bath. After that, I went to bed after saying good night to my friend.

The next day, I got to the ministry of education at 10:50. I walked up to room 404 and went straight in before someone else did. The woman I handed my file to the previous day was not there yet. I pleaded with her colleague, a man who must have been in his mid 60s to check the records and see if my file had been recorded. He really looked tired and did things very sluggishly. He had wrinkles all over his face and all the veins in his arms could be seen. The hair on his head was very scanty and grey as was his beard. From the normal way of things, a man like that would have long been retired. But if he was still there, one did not need to look too far to get a reason why. He just reminded me of Pauline Cooks who worked in the Bamenda branch ministry of Basic Education where I was based. She was in reality close to seventy years old but still in active service. She had gone to some men who could fake birth certificates and had one established for herself after paying an amount to them. Her intention was to work in the public service for much longer than the age of 55 years for women stipulated by the law. It was that fake birth certificate which she used to find her way into the public service. She was sluggish and old and spent most of her time dozing on the table in her office. There were moments she did not even go to work because age and old age crisis were weighing her down. Getting herself around sometimes was a very difficult task. But on paper, she was much younger than her first child Natalie and less than 55 years which did not permit her to retire. She became ineffective but was earning a full salary doing next to no work. It was obvious that the old man in that office that morning was in the same pot of soup. He asked me what my name was and I took out my identity card and handed to him. It took him quite some time to put on his lenses, read my name on the identity card and move to the desk of his absent colleague to open the record book. Flipping through the pages of the thick book was yet another task but at last he told me that my name was in the register. That meant that my documents were to be forwarded to the next level. With that certainty in mind, I decided to head to Patience Travel Agency where I booked for the 14:00 bus. Since my friend, Jacob was at work, I decided to remain at the travel agency and rang him instead. I informed him of what I saw at the ministry and told him I would call him when I got back to my home town.

The bus took off at 14:15 to cover the 313 kilometres from the nation's capital to Bamenda Town. People spoke less and the noises one got were those made by the bus engine and the radio. When we got to Kenkem, a small town midway between the capital of the nation and Bamenda town, everyone expected the driver to make a stop over there for people to either ease themselves or buy food to eat or take back home. He did not and even the plea of some women passengers was not enough to make him change his mind. Some of the women, out of frustration, decided to rain insults on him. He seemed to have been a patient man and a 'John stone' as he remained silent and concentrated on the road ahead of him.

We entered Bamenda Town at 20:20 and as we drove on to the travel agency premises, Mr. Kiamba, the owner, was there to welcome his passengers back. He was a very strict man and did not want anything that could make his customers unhappy. He knew the passengers were the most important element of his business. For that reason he was very sensitive to any criticisms anyone made and did everything possible to weed out problems as soon as they cropped up. That day was no exception. He got negative answers as he sought to know from the passengers if they had a nice trip. When he asked what went wrong, the women who would have loved to pick up one or two things at Kenkem told him of what the driver did. He immediately called the attention of the driver in a very commanding tone.

"I do not pay you only to take my bus and bring it back in good condition. I pay you to make my passengers happy. I'm not saying that you should turn the bus into a cab by stopping anyhow or anywhere in the name of making people happy. You were driving on the highway and should have stopped at Kenkem without them even asking you to do so. Now, I want you to get back on that steering wheel and take these good customers back to Kenkem so that they can eat and buy whatever they would have wanted to," he ordered.

Those who were still descending from the bus hurried out after hearing what the Boss said. I couldn't tell if he meant what he said or if he was just employing the tactics of a politician. But what was clear was that no one was prepared to undertake the trip again to Kenkem just to eat or buy a few items. The idea was unreasonable. Whatever the intentions of the Boss I think he succeeded in putting smiles on the faces

27

of the passengers. Even if anyone of them had planned on not coming to the travel agency because of the actions of the driver, what his Boss just did was enough to make him or her revisit their decision. I left the agency and headed straight home where I had a bath and went to bed. I called my friend Paul to inform him that I was back in town and we planned on meeting two days later.

On Friday, Feb. 28th, I got to my friend's house at 11:50. He was not in but his wife and two children as well as the babysitter were in. Paul's wife who was heavily pregnant sat in the sitting room with the two kids while the babysitter was in the kitchen doing something, probably preparing lunch. I joined them in the sitting room and we sat watching TV and conversing. At 12:15 her phone which was on the table started ringing. Since it was much closer to me, I picked it up and handed to her. On the screen I could read 'Heart Attack Calling.' It was indeed her husband, Paul who was calling. His name kept changing in her phone depending on the atmosphere reigning in the house. Whenever she had a problem with her husband, his name in her phone was either 'Heart Attack' or 'High Blood.' When things were smooth, his name in the phone was 'Honey' or 'Sweet Heart.' I could read from the 'Heart Attack calling' that their relationship, at that moment, was not at its best. She answered the call and told her husband that I was around waiting for him. I could not help feeling for her as her pregnancy was at a critical stage and stress was the last thing she needed. I asked her what the matter was and she pleaded with me to talk to my friend about his womanizing attitude. She complained of her husband leaving the house too early and returning very late. I told her that leaving the house and coming back late did not mean that my friend was spending his time with another woman. She saw it as my attempt to defend him but I urged her to keep such thoughts out of her mind. But I promised to talk to my friend not only about his attitude but her state as well.

At 12:45 Paul came in and we all moved to the dining table for lunch. While we ate he asked me to accompany him somewhere to recover some money which someone borrowed from him. I asked him if there was a dog there and he said that there was not. He had already noted that I always asked that question each time he asked me to accompany him somewhere and wanted his curiosity satisfied.

"But why do you always ask if there are dogs any where I ask you to accompany me?" he asked. "If I can remember, this is the third or fourth time I'm asking you to accompany me and you keep asking if there are dogs there. What do you have against dogs?

"Do you really want to know? I asked.

"Yes, of course. That is the reason why I asked?" he responded.

I reflected for a while and then my thoughts settled on Coco. The ordeal Coco subjected me came back to mind as if it happened the previous day. "It was in 1988, when I was ten years old," l began. "I had two friends that I did all the good and bad things with. They were Ibrahim and Peter. Can you still remember them?"

"Yes of course," he said. "And so...?"

"We were inseparable," I went on. "So, one fateful Sunday, my parents left the house and went for our village meeting leaving me in the house. Peter and Ibrahim came over and we decided to make something like a wooden 'car' with the shaft of modern cars as its tires. Three of them were needed. We rushed to my father's little garage where he kept his little spare parts and got them there. Two were put behind and one in front. The one in front had to be flexible because it had to function as the steering wheel. It could easily roll on tar and smooth surfaces. Only one person could sit on it at a time and another person had to act as the engine pushing from behind. After making our car, the yard of my family compound was not good enough for testing it as it was not sloppy enough. I immediately suggested to my two friends that we carry it to the Cathedral premises which were well tarred and sloppy too. They bought my idea and we carried our car on our heads in turns and went to the church premises. The church yard extended right to the main road used by heavy and light vehicles. The distance from the church building to the main road was about 500 meters. It was a good distance for any of us who were in the 'car' to really enjoy the ride. Whenever any of us got to the point where the car could no longer go further, we got up and carried it on our heads and walked back to the point of departure which was at the main door into the cathedral. It was Peter who went first in the testing exercise. While he was in the 'car', Ibrahim and I pushed and let go when we were sure that it had gathered enough speed. Ibrahim was next and I was the last. After the testing exercise it was time for each and everyone to give his impressions. We unanimously decided that the 'car' was good. With the testing exercise over, it was time to enjoy the ride even more. Ibrahim went first while Peter went after he returned. It was my turn to go after peter returned with the car on his head. When I sat in it, I concentrated in front while waiting for them to push me as I did when it was their turn. I could feel that there was something like a hand which held me on my shoulder but would not push even when I insisted. I got angry and accused my friends of being unfair and angrily turned round to face them. What I saw was neither Ibrahim nor Peter but a big dog which looked like a young horse. My friends were nowhere to be found. It was difficult to tell whether they evaporated or the earth opened its mouth and swallowed them up. Anyway, that was not my main concern at that particular moment. What was more important was getting out of the jaws of Coco. Whether it was fate or design, the 'car' started rolling down. I controlled it as best as I could and Coco soon let go of me as the 'car' gathered speed though he didn't stop chasing me. As naïve as I was, I would have sat in the 'car' until it hit the main road and I'm sure Coco would have turned back. Instead, I sprang to my feet immediately I sensed that there was a small distance separating me from Coco. Of course, he caught up with me in the twinkle of an eye and held me by the arm of the red pullover I had on. I wrestled with it and it had to let go of my pullover. After that it did not try to hold any part of my attire again. Instead it guarded me, making sure that I did not try to run away. That Coco certainly had the brain of a human being. It was as though it could read my mind and knew the next move I was planning. I tried every tactic anybody with the brain of a ten-year old child could imagine. Any direction I headed to or even thought of heading to, Coco was there before me. I felt like a sinner in the hands of an angry God. Mark you; I did all that shouting at the top of my voice. With all my attempts at getting away from Coco having failed, I soon realized amidst my desperation that all that shouting was not going to lead me anywhere. So, I resorted to some diplomacy. First, I went down on my one knee and begged Coco. That did not move him one bit. I persisted and even promised to bring my share of meat as well as the fattest bone whenever my mother

31

returned from the market for him to enjoy. That too didn't work. I stopped crying and began to wonder what Coco was going to do to me. Just when I thought there was no salvation and my fate was sealed, I saw someone standing on the steps leading up to the church house. It was Fr. Francis, the parish priest. I immediately began to run towards him. Coco did not try to stop me but was moving slowly behind making sure that the gap between us did not widen. When I attempted to deviate from the path leading to Fr. Francis, Coco grabbed me by the pullover and brought me back on the right track. I knew there was no need trying to escape and walked straight to the priest. When I got to him, he asked me to go and carry the 'car' right down near the main road and bring it to him. My 'bodyguard' accompanied me. When I was getting close to my wooden car, Coco passed in front only to make sure that I did not seize the opportunity to get away. I lifted it and placed on my head and started walking back towards the priest with Coco guarding me from behind. I got to him and he took my wooden car and put it in the open back of his Toyota Hilux. He opened the passenger door, lifted me and put me inside the vehicle. He got behind the steering wheel and started driving out of the church premises. I knew he was taking me home since he knew my parents and where I lived. On the way, he asked a good number of questions but I did not answer any. What annoyed me was that he asked the questions laughing. That was clear proof that he must have derived a lot of pleasure from seeing Coco torment me the way it did.

"What explanation did your friends give you as to how they managed to escape?" Paul asked.

"They told me that Coco surprised them when they were focused on pushing me. Since they started running in separate directions, it was difficult for Coco to chase and catch everyone. I was the only one who had not discovered that it was there and became an easy prey. By the time I realized what was happening, I was already in Coco's grip," I replied.

My story provoked a lot of laughter. Paul's wife laughed the most. Paul asked me if my parents caned me when the priest took me back home. My response was that the priest got home when my parents were not in. They only returned shortly after he left. I don't know if they ever knew of the incident. But from that day I started being scared of dogs. Paul then asked if it was only that single incident which soured my relationship with dogs. My response was negative but I had to keep the story of my next ordeal for some other day.

It was 13:40 when we left the dining table. We went and sat in the sitting room watching TV until 14:00 when we decided to leave Paul's house.

"Mammy Sheila (mother of Sheila), we are going out" he told his wife as we made our way out. Sheila was the name of their first daughter.

"Is that what you call your wife? Why don't you look for a pet name which is modern, romantic and smooth?" I asked.

"So, people who don't have wives know how to call wives eeh!" he retorted.

"Look my friend, the fact that I'm not yet married does not mean I'll remain single all my life. When I finally do, I will give her a beautiful pet name and not your local 'Mammy Sheila'", I told him.

"Well, I'll be seriously waiting for that day," he retorted again. Once out of his yard, I asked him where exactly we were going and he told me that it was to Mr. Kengo's house which was some 15 kilometres from where we stood in the outskirts on the eastern part of town. I then drew his attention to the delicate state of his wife. I was very careful not to let him know that I had earlier discussed anything with her. I told him that with his wife in the state she was in, she needed him around most of the time. He stared at me with a queer expression on his face which made me uncomfortable. 'What do you know about family life?' was probably the question he wanted to ask me with such an expression. He told me that his wife was hell each time she was pregnant.

"She rains all sorts of insults on me and sees me as the source of all her misfortune. The irony is that she does not want me to leave her side but when I'm by her, she makes my life miserable. She would say that she wants to eat this or that and I would go for it. When I've brought it, she would say that she does not want it and would request something else. Only someone with metallic nerves can tolerate all that. I just can't. It has become so unbearable that I have decided to leave the house very early and return only when it is time to go to bed. That way she does not torture me too much," he explained.

I pleaded with him to revise his strategy as women had their own way of thinking. He asked me what I meant and I explained to him that his wife might have been attributing his long hours outside to having a concubine. I added that if that was the case, it was better to avoid anything which could stress her out. I further urged him to take the insults until their baby was born. He agreed with me and said that he was going to bear any torments from his wife for the sake of his unborn baby but vowed never to go in for another. I laughed and told him that the decision not to have more children was not his to make but hers. All in all, I was happy with his resolution because it was the first time he admitted something

I said without reminding me that I did not belong to the circle of married couples. He made my stomach revolt each time he remarked that I belonged to the circle of bachelors each time I brought up or tried to give advice on family life.

4

Just then a cab was about to pass us when Paul stopped it with a show of hand. Paul told the driver our destination and he agreed to take us there. We jumped in and joined some two other passengers who were in the cab. About 500 meters from where we entered, we drew closer to a check point. Four policemen manned it. One of them stepped forward with a whistle in his mouth and raised his right hand signalling that we should halt. Everybody in the cab sighed except one. The cab driver halted some seven meters after the check point. We expected him to remain behind his steering wheel and wait for the police officer who stopped him to walk up to him. But he was the one who took out a 500 francs note from his shirt pocket and slipped it inside his car documents and went out to meet the policeman. That was not normal. He did not carry overload as was the case with most cab drivers. Those drivers who left their cars to go and meet highway policemen were those that knew the legal rules but decided to break them deliberately by either not having all required car documents or carrying overload. Even if he was not in order somewhere, we considered that it was still not normal for the cab driver to leave his steering wheel. Doing that was an indication that there was already some kind of treaty between them to break the laws of the land for self interest while the nation suffered. However, the only guy who did not sigh when we grinded to a halt wanted to prove his point.

"I don't see why you all sighed when we halted a while ago. It is through the presence of those brave men on the road that stolen vehicles are recovered and contraband goods are seized," he said.

My friend, Paul, was not happy with that explanation and burst out in anger.

"What are you talking about?" he asked. "Did I hear you say that they recover stolen vehicles and catch contraband goods? Young man, you give us the impression that you do not live in this country or you are from another planet. Didn't you see what that driver did with the 500 francs note he took out of his pocket? Do you think that policeman has taken those car documents because he is interested in them? He has taken them because he knows he would find that money in there. Leaving that one aside, how long have we been standing here? Has any of them come to see what that driver is transporting in the booth of this car? How then would they know if the car is a stolen one or not or if it is transporting contraband goods? They are only interested in the bribes or little money they can extort from innocent drivers. Honestly I don't know their use."

"You cannot say that they have no use. That is an over-statement," the police defender reacted. "At least we enjoy some degree of peace and security thanks to them."

That further explanation coming from the police defender did appear to have angered my friend even more. I think if he had something like a good stick or any other weapon, he would have landed it on that young man's head.

"Young man, I have the firm conviction that you are benefiting from the chaos in this country. Why are you defending them? Do you know how it hurts for you to labour hard for something and at the end someone else comes and takes it away without bothering to know how much you laboured for it? Do you know how it feels when armed robbers come into your house, steal your property, rape your wife or daughter before your very eyes and you can't do anything?" Paul asked.

The young man remained speechless. Paul paused for a while and I saw his eyes water with tears.

"Maybe, your father is one of those ministers who has built mansions and bought big cars with stolen money which you are enjoying and can afford to make such careless statements", he resumed. "I know that their principal mission is to provide security for people and goods. But they had abdicated that responsibility a long time ago. Now, what do they do? They extort money from poor civilians, take bribes from innocent drivers, use live bullets on armless civilians and peaceful demonstrators and worst of all, the regime in place uses them to suppress us. Apart from all that, what else do they know? Do you know why the population of this town has resorted to burning thieves to death when they lay their hands on them? It is because they will catch thieves or armed robbers today and hand them over to the police and the next day they will be back in the streets. It is even rumoured that some of them provide the robbers with the weapons they use to operate so that they can share the booties after successful operations. Besides, call them at midnight and tell them that you are being robbed. They will tell you that they do not have fuel or that they cannot locate your residence or they'll ask you if the thieves are armed or to cut long stories short, they will tell you that they're on their way and will arrive only at 06:00 the next day" he said.

"Sir, I agree with almost all of what you have said but I don't think there is anything you or I can do about the situation. We can only leave it to God", said the other passenger who sat next to the police defender.

"Just listen to what you are saying", Paul interrupted him. "I think that is the mentality that the majority of us have and the authorities have mastered that so well. Your friend there talked about peace. There is peace because the people of this country are cowards who cannot fight for their rights. Instead of rising up and fighting for what they believe in as one man, they prefer to drown their frustrations in alcohol. The authorities have understood that and are making sure it is always available. We have beer parlours every 50 meters in this town and all over the country. They will accept to sponsor any research you want to carry out only if it has to do with alcohol. We have sold our freedom for alcohol. That is the reason why I sometimes hate this country and regret why I had to leave Europe to come back here. There, if you are in trouble and see a policeman, you know you are safe. But here, if you are in trouble and see a policeman, you have to run away instead. He might pretend to protect you but he could be doing so calculating what he can gain or make out of you. I thought I was coming home but I was coming to hell" he concluded.

Just then, the cab driver returned and we hit the road again. Paul immediately turned his attention to him.

"I saw you giving your car documents to that policeman. Did he check if everything was ok?" Paul asked.

"Ha ha ha!" the driver laughed. "Who told you they are interested in checking documents? Is that one even able to read or write? He is interested in the 500 Frs. I put inside," he said.

"Did you give him that money because your documents are not in tact?" Paul asked.

"I have all the necessary documents. I gave it because it is like a "daily contribution" and I wanted to save time" he explained.

"What do you mean?" Paul asked.

"I mean it does not matter if my documents are ok or not. If I don't give them, they can decide to keep me there just to waste my time for no good reason. So, I have to give it so that they can let me go. You know with us, time is money. The boss has a specific amount he is expecting from me at the end of the day. Do you expect me to go and tell him I was tied down by a policeman? He will not listen to me and might fire me instantly for not playing the national game like others," he said.

Paul turned to the police defender to use the cab driver's explanation to buttress his point that police officers were useless. The young man remained speechless until finally he alighted without saying another word. I guess his silence meant that he was already psychologically defeated.

I really wondered if the young man knew the truth but was deliberately refusing to acknowledge it. That kind of reasoning was common with those who were in power or those who were economically comfortable. Because they were okay, they often sounded as though everybody in the country that fine. The ministers could not make a complete sentence without making reference to the head of state who appointed them ministers. They always referred to the relative peace in the country as the government's and particularly the head of state's greatest achievement. They were comfortable with the huge pay packages and numerous other benefits they enjoyed. But within the common man in the street whose daily life and existence remained a permanent battle for survival, anger was boiling when those in high places talked of peace. How could they be talking of peace and prosperity when there was too much poverty around while at the same time they arrogantly displaying stolen wealth around the place in the form of expensive cars? I could understand my friend's outburst.

That notwithstanding, 40 minutes after we left Paul's house, we got to GRA. It was a neighbourhood inhabited only by public sector workers. They did not have to pay physical cash to anyone or a bank account at the end of each month because the money was deducted directly from their pay packages. Paul soon asked the cab driver to stop and we got out after Paul settled him.

"That is Mr Kengo's house over there", Paul told me pointing to it.

The house Mr Kengo's lived in was a very simple one with a very large yard in front. Cypress trees were planted all round the house and it served as a fence. There was a gate made of wood and old corrugated iron sheets. The gate was some 50 meters from the main road and some 10 meters from the house. The house was identical to many others around. Since the gate was open, we decided to walk right in. But when we were about three meters from the main door into the house, we could hear noises coming from within. The noises indicated that people were fighting with weapons which might have been household utensils. Our suspicions were confirmed when one of the missiles which was a shoe, landed on the window frame and shattered a few blades. We thought it was a general family fight between the man of the house and the rest of his family. We rushed in cautiously to intervene. But when we got into the house cautious not to receive any on coming missiles, it was not Mr. Kengo fighting with his family but he was fighting with a much younger man. They had sacked the whole house and from first view, one would have had the impression that a hurricane just swept through it. The two men were at one end of the house trying to inflict as much pain as they could on each other. I grabbed the much younger man who was on Mr. Kengo landing punches and pulled him off. My friend on his part grabbed Mr. Kengo who was seemingly still thirsty for more fight though physically he was not looking too good. He was still trying to take advantage of the fact that I held his opponent to inflict more pain on him but my friend stopped him.

"Gentlemen, I don't think fighting has ever solved any problem," Paul said. "Why don't you sit down as the gentlemen that you are and sort out your differences through dialogue?

"That fool is not a gentleman and I think the only language he understands is that of the fist," the young man said.

"If you call me a fool again, I will give you the beating of your life," Mr Kengo warned.

Paul and I were eager to know the bone of contention between them.

"What could really push two grown people to be behaving like wild animals in the bush? What is going on?" Paul asked.

"That old fool has lived his life and does not want me to live mine. He would not allow me to enjoy the woman I love alone. I never came to share his wife with him and I don't know why he is sharing mine with me. He is only using her and would never take her even as a second wife. She does not hesitate to compare him to me whenever we have our differences. She considers him a real man though he looks old," he said crying.

I felt sorry for him as I could see how hurt he was. It was obvious that he truly loved the woman he was alluding to and engaging Mr. Kengo in a serious fight was a desperate attempt to save his love. I would have done the same thing just as anybody else.

"You are not man enough. You are much younger and anybody would have expected to hear me say that my woman is flirting with someone much younger but it is the other way round. Instead of feeling cheated on, you should try to see where you are lacking and work hard to fill the gaps. Those gaps shall always make a woman run away. If it was not me, it would have been someone else. So, you are supposed to be thanking me for helping you realize your shortcomings instead of fighting me. Do you think landing punches is what will make you a man? Josephine fell for me because she started having the impression that she was dating another woman who is here trying to prove to me that he is a man by flexing his muscles," Mr Kengo said.

"It is because of the money you shower on young girls that they tend to under look us, the young men. It has become so common to see a sixteen years old girl going out with a man old enough to be her grandfather. In the villages and village schools, there are very high rates of teenage pregnancies . Do you think the teenage girls are impregnated by young men like us? Of course not….they are impregnated by the likes of that fool who are already one leg in the jaws of death but still want to hang on to life. They flatter the children with the pensions they earn and in return, load the children with babies. That is not the only bad thing….they help in the spreading of this deadly disease called HIV/AIDS. I think people like this old fool here are a threat to the future generation and should be cleaned like germs," the young man said.

Though the battle had changed from the physical exchange of punches to verbal attacks, Paul and I were not happy with some of the comments especially those which were made by Mr. Kengo. He was already an old man who had already lived his life, had his children and was still happily married. There was no need for him to prevent others from also living their lives. If there was a total stranger there, it was me and I felt that I had no right to start giving moral lessons there. So, I let my friend do all the talking as we reasoned almost in the same way.

"Mr. Kengo, if there was a judge here, he or she would not favour you. Our people say that a man cannot give birth to a son and then place a rock on his head. That means that you are not supposed to give birth to a child and prevent the child from growing. You do not want this young man to grow and fighting with him over his woman is ardent testimony to that fact. Fighting with him here indicates that you do not see him as a son and I don't think you would want to engage a fight with any of your grown sons over a woman. How then would the young ones grow if the older generation deliberately refuses to grow old? Please, life has been so kind to you and you are lucky to have found a job in the public service and are still working. It is not because you have some money that you think you should use it in frustrating the lives of others. What you have been accused of is punishable by divine law. What would be your benefit if you gain all the skirts in the world and lose your soul?" Paul said.

We got there to ask for a debt but ended up being peace makers. Paul was not going to be a good peace maker if he did not point out the short comings of both parties. So, after telling Mr. Kengo what he thought was inappropriate in his behaviour, he turned to the young man.

"Where did you keep your manners? Are you supposed to be exchanging punches with someone old enough to be your father? We all agree that what he did was mean and any judge would condemn him for it. But society would frown at you, a young man, for engaging Mr. Kengo in a physical fight no matter what he did wrong. Just look at all the damage you've caused in here. Do you think the law will favour you for coming from outside and doing this in another man's house even if your case is a genuine one? If you are asked to pay for all this damage, would you be able to? Please, let's always try to think before acting," my friend said.

It would appear the words of my friend completely weakened the spirits of the two wrestlers. The young man decided to leave not after telling his rival that things were going to be worse if he was seen loitering just three hundred meters around where his woman was. However, with just three of us in the house, the disorder was staring us in the face. We had to put some order there before settling down on the debt asking mission that took us there in the first place. We did and carried out the shattered pieces of window blades before someone got his or herself wounded by them. One curious thing was that no member of Mr. Kengo's family was around. Paul and I wondered where they were and sought to know. He told us that they all went out to visit a relative. I was certain that his family would have been in disarray if the cuckolded young man got there when they were all at home. His wife would not have taken it lightly. But since our principal target was debt recovery, Paul went straight to it. In response, Mr. Kengo started by thanking us for helping to put his house back in order but was sorry to tell my friend that he was not in possession of the 30.000 francs at that moment because of some family matters. But he promised to give the money at the end of that month which was still some two weeks away. My friend did not insist but told him that he did not want to be the one to come for it again. Mr. Kengo promised to bring it to my friend's house once he took his salary. We allowed him to nurse his wounds and left but wondered what kind of story he was going to hatch to convince his family when they returned.

When we got back to the highway, my friend told me that he had no money and had to find some since he had a family. I too did not have enough to spare any. So, I waited to hear him say what he intended to do next.

"Since I've not succeeded in getting that 30.000 from Mr. Kengo, I will have to go to the central post office to get some money from my savings account which will sustain me for the rest of these two weeks. Would you like to accompany me there?" he asked.

"Well, I have nothing doing till tomorrow. Sure, I will," I told him.

"Then what are we waiting for? Let's go," he said.

We boarded a cab en route for the post office.

5

We got in front of the central post office twenty minutes after leaving Mr. Kengo's house. We alighted from the taxi and moved directly into the post office building. It was crowded inside. Some people were busy buying postage stamps while others cued up to make cash withdrawals from their accounts. We decided to sit down on one of the benches in front of the large counter to wait for the cue to reduce. Less than 15 minutes inside the post office, some four armed men who were dressed in black and also wore masks made their entrance. Two stood by the door while the other two went close to the counter. One of them fired a warning shot at one of the bulbs with a silencer and ordered all of us to go to sleep. Paul went down from the bench onto the floor with his head in the direction of the counter. I got up from where I sat, backed the counter before going down on the floor. I laid flat on my stomach with my hands on my head like all the rest in the post office. With my head in the opposite direction of the counter, I was able to lift my head a little to see what was going on at the counter through the two large mirrors which stood on the right and left side of the main door which led in and out of the post office. Through both mirrors one could see all that went on inside the post office. Another armed robber handed a little traveller's bag to one of the cashiers behind the counter and asked her to load it. Gripped by fear especially as the robber pointed the barrel of the Kalashnikov at her, she obeyed without any resistance. But it seemed she had fear only for the gun and not fear to steal. She stuffed some bank notes in her breast ware but unfortunately some edges of the bank notes could be seen. That of course drew the attention of the armed robber who gave her the bag and that was when I raised my head a little and saw it too.

"Hey young lady, what do you think you are doing? Put everything inside," the armed robber ordered.

"Yes sir," she obeyed in fear as she pulled out those from her breast ware and dropped them in the bag as well. Just as a thief wouldn't want to see another thief or be robbed by another thief, the robber saw a rival in the lady behind the counter. He was not at all happy and so moved even closer to her with the gun pointing at her.

"I hate stealing," he said threateningly. "Give me that bag and come out here.

The young lady obeyed and was asked to lie down like the rest of us. Since she loved her dear life, she still obeyed. In four minutes, they had completed their operation and jumped into a waiting 504 Peugeot car outside. Everybody got up after the last armed robber went out through the door. Those of us who were caught inside saw only four armed men but it became obvious after they left that there were others outside.

"Is everybody alright? Was anybody hurt? What will I do with my sick child in the hospital? How do I pay my weekly contributions?" Those were some of the questions people asked when the robbers left. Many people walked out of the post office quietly, panic stricken and trembling. I did not think they went back to their daily activities. Most people simply went home. The ordeal was certainly too much for the nerves of so many people to bear.

However, Paul and I did not leave the post office as many people did. We went and remained outside the building to see what would happen next. We expected something to happen and indeed it happened. A police van pulled up in front of the post office 30 minutes after the armed bandits had left. There was an outburst of laughter from the crowd outside.

"See when they are coming", said one bystander.

"If it is to take bribe or extort money from tourists, they will be very swift but when it comes to fighting off criminals and protecting innocent people, they are never less than two hours late. I don't know why they call the bandits criminals instead of colleagues whereas they all specialise in reaping where they did not sow," said another.

They did not hear any of those comments as they were still further from those who made them. They got out of their van well armed and the first thing they did was seal off the area. They did not allow anyone to go in or out of the post office building. Some of them went in, while others remained out. The police boss was the last person to get out of the van and he went straight into the post office building. He re-emerged just less than ten minutes later. It seemed he did not get answers to his questions and decided to come out to get answers from those who were outside.

"Who was in there when those thieves were operating here?" he asked.

Nobody indicated and he turned to walk back in when I stopped him.

"Were you in there when those criminals attacked?" he asked.

"Yes I was", I replied.

"What did you see?" he asked next.

"Only the ceramic tiles on the floor", I replied.

"Stupid, that is not what I mean. Did you see any of their faces?" he asked again seemingly annoyed.

"How could I see any of their faces when my face was glued to the floor?" I asked getting annoyed too. "Your post is just 600 meters from here and those guys came and successfully carried money away and you couldn't do anything about it. Now that they have successfully gone away, you are here insulting me as if I am responsible for what just happened. You know what, you are just a bunch of mediocre policemen and it would not surprise me if you were promoted to a higher rank after this incident."

"Hey!!! Watch your mouth. I can order your arrest and detention right away", he threatened and went into the post office.

The crowd cheered and jeered as we argued. When he turned his back, the crowd cheered and cheered even more. They considered me a hero and I decided to go home afraid of getting into trouble. Paul was not very happy with my piece of drama with the police Boss.

"Do you know you have a very big mouth?" he reprimanded.

"Yes I do. In fact it is the only thing I can boast of", I fought back.

We decided to head to our various homes since there was a lot of nervousness and anxiety in and around the post office. I don't think the post office workers would have had the zeal to work after the nerve wrecking experience the armed robbers subjected them to. I would have just gone home if I was in their shoes.

I got home late that afternoon and could see from a distance that my door was open. Helen, my girlfriend stood by the door watching me as I walked in. I could smell a dead rat. I knew there was something eating her up and she must have been waiting for me to make a mistake so that she could use it to vent her anger out on me. She got her opportunity when on entering the house; I mistakenly pushed over a stool which was not well placed. She told me that other people stayed in their houses but I spent most of my time out with some cheap prostitutes. I did not know where she got such information from but I was definitely not happy with it and was not in the mood to quarrel with her that afternoon. I went in, had a bath and immediately left the house again. I did not tell her where I was going though she sat in the sitting room as I was leaving. That was what I did each time she wanted a confrontation. I was not married to her yet but sometimes she made me feel that she was too much for me to handle. Each time I thought of settling down with her, her sometime harsh way of dealing with situations made me think twice and I would give up the idea momentarily. Another thing I hated about her was the assumptions that spilled out of her mouth without any backing. All those made me scared that things could be a lot worse once her feet were firm in my house. But you would certainly want to know why I remained with her despite her hard character. Well, the truth was that I loved her and she was the devil I knew. I loved it as she did not hide the rough side of herself. That made me more conscious of what I was getting into if at the end of the day I decided to be her husband.

Nevertheless, I got to the main road from where I boarded a taxi to Uncle Joe's house which was situated some seven kilometres still within town from where I lived. I got there while he was not at home. But his wife and four children were there. I met her in the sitting room in a very pensive mood. She was so engrossed by her thoughts that she did not see me walk in. I called her the way her children did as a sign of respect. I asked what she was thinking of and she

53

told me that she was worried about the direction her marriage was taking.

"I now quarrel most of the time with your uncle," she told me.

I had an idea of relationship crisis and imagined what she must have been going through as she was already married. I tried to offer some comforting words.

"All marriages experience crises at one time or another and yours is no exception. I know the crises are just temporary but they are not supposed to break up your marriage. The crises are needed in your marriage because you are supposed to take advantage of them to renew your marriage vows. If two brothers or sisters from the same womb could quarrel and fight, what more of you, two total strangers from different homes, backgrounds and even culture?" I asked.

She listened and sighed but didn't say anything. She just sat staring at me. I tried to imagine the gloomy world she had in her mind. It was terrible to imagine that what one had spent perhaps years to build was going to crumble and I did not blame her for feeling desperate. She soon left me and went to the kitchen to prepare the evening meal. I remained in the sitting room watching TV while the children remained outside playing.

At 19:00 my uncle walked in and greeted me. He heard noise in the kitchen and knew his wife was there but did not bother to go and chat or say some nice words to her as I've always known him to do when things were fine. He moved straight to their bedroom and remained there. When it was time for dinner, his wife sent Sandra, their second daughter to go and call for daddy. She soon returned with information that daddy was on his way. But he emerged only an hour later. He did not go to the table but moved to where I was and sat on the chair opposite me. His wife went to the room after saying goodnight to me. When she left, my uncle sought to know how I was doing as well as my relationship with Helen. I did not want to beat around the bush. I told him of our woes, which was the reason why I was at his house. He gave me some advice on how to go about solving my problem with Helen.

"To assert your authority, you have to be tough on women," he said. "They are like children and if you are not tough, they will get out of hand and will ride you like a horse. You don't need to be sentimental.

I wanted to tell him that his way of reasoning was too old fashioned. But something prevented me from doing so. Maybe it was the fear of being mocked by him if I tried to tell him how modern men were supposed to behave with their wives. He would have certainly reminded me that I ran away from a problem in my house to come to his. To avoid the embarrassment, I just accepted everything he said though I did not agree with his problem solving strategy. He then asked me if I was going to spend the night at his place and I accepted.

It was 22:15 when I walked to the guest room where I had to spend the night. I laid on the bed but could not find sleep. There were so many things on my mind and the greatest one was Helen. I didn't know what to do to convince her to stop suspecting me. I hated her so much each time she accused me of dating other girls. At midnight, I could still hear some noise in the sitting room. The TV was still on and I suspected that my uncle had no intention of sleeping in the same room with his wife that night. I got out of the room and walked to the sitting room where I found him dead asleep. I shook him and asked him to go to bed. He told me that he was ok where he was. It was then I decided to be very frank with him.

"A few hours ago, you were giving me lessons on how to solve problems with my girlfriend. Helen is just my girlfriend but Elizabeth is your wife and mother of your children. Can't you try to solve whatever problems you have with her even for the sake of your children? Being tough is good when you want to assert your authority but it is better placed in an employer-employee relationship. That is not the situation here. We are talking about your family here. Being tough with a woman because you are afraid that she might ride you as a horse is too old fashioned," I told him bluntly.

My criticism made him more alert. He got up and sat properly.

"You are now criticising my methods and if you are doing that it means you know better than me. But you ran away from a problem similar to mine and have come to hide here," he said.

"I knew you were going to say that. If I criticise your method, it does not mean that I know better. All I'm saying is that the days when women were just to be seen and not heard, now belong to the past. We are now in a different era and our mentalities have to evolve with it. You have to sometimes go down on your knees for peace to reign in your home even if you are not the cause of the problem," I explained.

He stared at me with an open mouth. I was like a sort of superman from outer space who was saying extra ordinary things not good for the ears.

"From where did you learn such things?" he asked.

56

"It doesn't matter," I said. "I think that once in a while you should inject new ideas into those old ideas of yours. In the days of old, it was a normal thing to beat your wife like a child or a thief. Today it is almost a taboo. Anyone who sees you doing such a thing today would call you uncivilized. So, please uncle the fact that I ran from my home does not mean I should not have a say as far as resolving matrimonial problems are concerned. Who stands to gain if things are fine here and who stands to lose if things fall apart? It is you and your entire family. So, do me a favour; I don't care to know the nature of your problem or who started it or who did what. I want you to go in there, wake Elizabeth up and talk things out. You were supposed to give me that kind of advice if I found myself in a similar situation but I'm the one giving it to you. What are you doing still sitting there?" I asked.

Uncle Joe did not move. He did not say anything either. He just sat there staring at me without blinking. I equally had my eyes fixed on him without blinking. I took it as a contest to see who would withdraw first. He was the first to take his eyes off me and started staring at the floor. Full of confidence that I had won a psychological battle, I stood up without taking my eyes off him. He remained staring at the floor for about three minutes. When he raised his head and looked again into my eyes, I told him I was waiting. Without wasting any more time, he left for the room. It was 02:05 by my watch. I then turned off the TV and went to my room.

6

The next morning, I got out of bed at 07:30 and met my uncle and his family already having breakfast at the table. It was the perfect family I always met whenever I visited them. I smiled and stared at my uncle as I walked towards them to say good morning. Madam and husband were all smiles as they sat next to each other. I then went to the bathroom to wash up before joining them at table.

After breakfast, it was time for my uncle to go to work. He said goodbye to his wife and children and I followed him out. I asked how he felt that morning. He did not hide his feelings and thanked me for coming to hide in his house. We soon parted as he boarded a taxi bound for work while I went back to his house. I stayed there until 10:00 when I decided to go back to my own house.

It took me 45 minutes to get back to my house because I decided to go on foot. I did so with the hope that Helen would not be home when I got there. I had no intention of confronting her. She was a thorn in my flesh even though she remained the devil I knew. I think heaven was on my side that day as I found no one at my house. I just went in and shut the door behind me. Since there was not much work to be done, I decided to catch up with some sleep first. My room became the most comfortable place at that moment and I had to make the most of it.

I woke up at 15:00, got out of the room and met Helen in the sitting room. She looked at me and did not utter a word. I could read only suspicion in her eyes. That did not bother me much as I was already used to it.

"Hi dear, how was your day?" I enquired.

Helen did not respond. I went out and sat on the steps that led into house. Helen did not follow me out but remained seated where I saw her. I sat there feeling a bit guilty for spending the night outside. I was undecided on whether to go in and tell her all that transpired the previous day or to just sit out there and see what she would do. I finally settled on the second option. I sat there and let my mind wander to what late Uncle Phil once told me about women.

"Son," he said. "One day you are going to be a man and people will judge you from the kind of family you will make. But women, you have to be very patient with them. Ah yes, patience... that is what many of you youths of today lack. Marriages in the 21st seem to have expiring dates. Divorce has become so fashionable. You have people who go to court today to sign for better and for worse and the very next day they are back there to file for divorce. In my days, that was an abomination. Listen my son, you will never find a perfect woman. A woman is like a wild wood in the forest which has not been tampered with. In that wild state you cannot do anything with it. So, you have to be like an artist who would get his tools and patiently carve out what he wants out of the wild wood. The tools you will use on a woman are patience, dialogue and most importantly love. Armed with such 'tools, you can then fashion out the woman of your dreams from the one that will come your way. No amount of prayers for a good wife will help you. A woman is a woman. The skin colour, origin, social status etc do not matter. So long as it is a woman, it will be the same enjoyment and the same trouble."

I was still buried in my thoughts when I heard Helen shouting at me.

"Have you become a day dreamer," she asked.

"What? Sorry I did not get what you said," I apologised.

"How would you hear when you are still thinking of the sweet night you had with I don't know whom," she said.

"What are you talking about?" I asked.

"You pretend as if you don't know what I'm talking about. Where did you sleep last night?" she asked.

"I spent the night at my uncle's place. Should I give you Uncle Joe's number so that you can call and verify?" I asked.

"No need for all that. He will obviously say 'yes' just to protect you. Leave the number. How do I know if you've not called him and you've both cooked up something in case I call to verify?" she asked.

I did not know if I should laugh or cry. I hated when I was speaking the truth and someone was there trying to make me look like a liar. Helen's comments pushed me to tell her my mind.

"Why are you tormenting me?" I asked. "As far as I know, I am not your husband. I am still a free man and free to do whatever I want with my life without having to render account to anyone. If you don't want to believe me when I say that I spent the night in my Uncle's house, then believe whatever you want," I told her and moved back to the sitting room.

She followed me.

"What do you mean? I'm I wasting my time here with you?" she asked with tears streaming down her eyes.

"I never said you were wasting your time. I'm just saying that I'm tired of you nagging me and always suspecting me. I now understand why some men spend most of their time in beer parlours whereas they have wives at home. Listen and listen carefully because I will not repeat it again. If I see a woman who would treat me better than you do, I will go for her without thinking twice," I warned.

I knew that was too severe and a blow to her pride. But I felt that I needed to be tough at that moment to put some things straight once and for all. I could read anger in her looks. She did not waste another minute. She grabbed her hand bag and ran out of the house crying. I remained glued to my seat. A feeling of guilt started building up in me. I wanted to run after her but resigned after a second thought. I had told her what was hurting me inside and there was no reason why I should have felt remorseful. Besides, if I told her how I felt, it was not because I hated her but because I wanted her to learn from her mistakes to be a better person. In addition, I knew that she was not perfect and I had to learn how to tolerate some of her shortcomings just as she had to tolerate some of mine if we were to be good and compatible partners. But her suspicions and nagging attitudes were just two I could not tolerate.

Still in my confusion and indecision, I saw her walk back in through the main door still crying. I looked at her but did not get off of my seat. Instead I began wondering why she came back. 'Is she coming back because she has realized the bad treatment she was meting out to me? Or is she coming back because she expected me to run after her and I did not? Or is she coming back because she is afraid that I might execute my threats of going after another if she left? There were only questions and no answers. But I knew only time was going to provide them.

"Smith, I'm so sorry if I'm treating you badly," she said still crying.

I did not react but remained where I was staring at her.

"Please Smith, don't you hear me? I said I'm sorry. Don't sit there just staring at me. Say something," she said with the crying gaining in intensity.

I got up and took her in my arms without still saying anything. The truth was that I did not know what to tell her.

"Smith, I love you so much. Only the thought of you in the arms of another woman tortures me to death. That's why I behave the way I do every time you come home late. Losing you is not my only worry. The high rate of insecurity scares me to death. I'm afraid something bad might happen to you. Early this morning I learnt of a robbery at the central post office which happened yesterday over the radio. With the high rate of insecurity in this town, I'm afraid of getting bad news in which you could be involved. That's why I always want you back home early. I might have been using the wrong methods which hurt you. Please I'm sorry. Forgive me," she apologised and continued sobbing.

Her mention of the post office robbery brought back vivid pictures of the incident to my mind. I wanted to tell her that I was among those trapped inside the post office at the time of the incident but did not after a second thought. I felt that telling her at that moment would be adding salt to injury. Besides, the tears running down her cheeks were tearing my heart into pieces though I was proving to be tough. Tears too had already built in my eyes and only the strength of the man in me prevented them from spilling out. I thought it was time to say something comforting.

"It's ok. I understand," I said with a lot of emotion in my voice and tears threatening to flow out. I still had her in my arms and she also held me tight. I could feel her tears wetting my shirt from my right shoulder. I could also feel her warm body and it grew warmer by the minutes. I started having some intense sensations running all over my body. My temperature started rising. It was as if my breath was going to cease though no one was strangling me. I felt her hand roll down my back. The sensation grew more intense and I held her even tighter as if I wanting her body to fuse completely with mine. My arms left her back and gradually moved to her breasts while my lips met her warm lips. Nothing in the world outside mattered at that moment. I found myself helpless in the face of my heart's desire. She let me explore her body and in the twinkle of an eye, we were on the floor. The to and fro movement was so intense. Her meaningless whispers urged me on. I felt heaven and wished it wouldn't end. But it did end and we both fell asleep after taking a bath.

It was 20:00 when we woke up. It was news time and we turned on the TV. She sat on my lap and we followed the news keenly.

"….. the police are presently searching for one Mr Kodjo Pierre, a secondary school teacher of government Secondary school Nyong. According to some twelve students who happen to be his, their parents gave them money which was intended to be their registration for the upcoming National Exams. Because the latest date was fast approaching and the cue in front of the principal's office was too long, the said Mr Kodjo came to them and asked them to let him assist them in the registration. Being their teacher, they had no reason to suspect him. They gave him their money and he took down their names. He then asked them to go back to class promising to bring the receipts to them there. He went back to them a few minutes later and told them that he had given the money to the principal and the principal had asked him to come for the receipts in an hour.

The students waited for more than an hour and their receipts were not forthcoming. They decided to go to the principal only to be informed that Mr Kodjo had not been seen in and around his office all day. Mr Kodjo was nowhere to be found. As we were leaving the school premises, there was lamentation and gnashing of teeth as the twelve students were wondering what they would tell their parents and where they would start searching for money to meet the deadline registration day which was the next day. In the meantime, information from Saker Street where Mr Kodjo lives says he was last seen at 13:30 today with a traveller's bag heading to an unknown destination. Affaire a suivre..."

Helen who was still sitting on my lap clapped her hands in total disbelief.

"Wonders shall never end!" she exclaimed. "Some people can be really heartless. If it was somebody who had never seen the four walls of a classroom, we might talk of eeeem… I don't know. But for a teacher who knows the importance of education to steal money from his own students, it is an abomination. He deserves the worst possible punishment."

"Well, he has betrayed the trust of his students which is bad. He has lied to them which is terrible. He has also played with their future which is horrible. But, that is not enough to condemn him or treat him as an outcast. I think we are condemning him too fast without finding out why he behaved the way he did," I said.

"Smith, you surprise me," she said.

"I'm only being objective. I am not defending him. What he did was very bad and should be punished. What I'm saying is that he is not the only guilty party in the matter. Our leaders only know how to say that 'teaching is a noble profession and teachers are nation builders'. They are nation builders with what resources? How much do teachers earn in this country? In one of my classes last week, I asked my students in Form Two how many of them would like to be teachers in the future. Out of a class of 96 students, do you know how many said they were going to be teachers? …Only one. I asked them why they did not like the teaching profession. Do you know what they told me? They said teachers are poor…. teachers don't dress well, etc .The state we are serving has turned us into slaves and beggars with the complicity of the IMF and The World Bank with their so called structural adjustment programs which are still to yield any fruits. Today they are talking of globalisation which is out to make us even poorer," I said.

Helen decided to leave my lap and move to the seat opposite the one I was sitting on. She maintained a fixed gaze on me which started making me uncomfortable.

"I'm not in any way trying to justify his actions. I'm just saying that we should not adopt the bad habit of judging and condemning people in a haste. Anyway, that was just my opinion. It is the job of the court to judge and sentence him. Please, stop staring at me like that," I said.

7

It was 21:00 when the news ended. We turned off the TV and went to bed. But before long I was fast asleep and my spirit went wandering. I soon found myself heading to a beautiful garden. The little road that led into it was tarred and lined with flowers on both sides. I saw a river which had all species of fish and sea mammals running not far from the garden. Out of the river came a mermaid who beckoned to me. I went very close to the river bank where she was. She offered me a fruit which I gratefully accepted. She said bye and went back into the river. I continued on my path and met a male lion which spoke to me in a gentle voice and also walked upright like a human being. Surprised to hear a lion speaking, I tried to run away.

"Come, do not be afraid. I'm not going to hurt you," he said. "Here, we live in harmony and look out for the wellbeing of one another. So, do not be afraid," he assured me. I summoned more courage and went closer to him.

"Where are you going to or who are you looking for?" he asked.

I was still surprised seeing him walking up right and talking and did not answer his question.

"I've told you not to be afraid. I'm only here to help you. I can take you to any where you want to go or take you to anyone you want to see. Here, I know everybody and everybody knows me," he explained.

"Well, I'm not here to see anyone in particular. I'm here for site seeing," I told him.

"In that case, I would like to invite you to my house. After exploring, just say 'Maine' and I'll be there, Ok?" he said.

I agreed and continued admiring the scenery. Monkeys and birds hung on trees and waved at me as I passed by. I felt loved and wanted as the inhabitants of the extensive garden welcomed me. '*This is where I love to be*', I said to myself as I moved along.

I soon came to a warehouse where I found someone who stood backing me. It was a lady.

"Hello," I called out.

She turned round and I recognised her as my late elder sister Irene who died in a fatal car accident when I was hardly six years old. She was not very excited to see me. She just stared at me for a few seconds and then turned and continued with what she was doing. She was gathering eggs and packing them in trays upon trays.

"What have you come to do here? I left you to take care of our younger ones and our parents when they grow old. With whom have you left them now that you are here," she asked.

I did not answer and instead wanted to know if I could eat some of the eggs.

"Yes, but on one condition: you must not take any along when you are going back. You can eat as much as you want but you cannot take any away," she reiterated.

"But why can't I take any along?" I asked.

"That is just the rule and you have to obey it without asking questions," she said sternly.

"In that case I will stay here with you so I can eat these nice eggs," I told her.

"No, you can't stay here with me. This is not a place for you," she said.

"Then let's go back together," I suggested.

"No, I can't come with you," she said already losing her patience.

"Why do you want to stay here all alone? Are all these eggs yours or you are working for somebody?" I asked.

"You ask too many questions. Whether they are mine or not is not your business. Just go back and take care of our family," she said.

"I will not go without you", I told her persistently.

"Smith, you are too stubborn. Just go and leave me alone" she said furiously.

"Ok, I will go but I must take some of these eggs with me", I said going to carry a tray of eggs.

"No please. No, no and no," she objected with all her strength.

Her objection did not mean anything to me as I was bent on taking some of the eggs back. I bent down to carry one tray when a good whip landed on my bag.

"Aaaaooooooouuuch!" I shouted and woke up.

"What is it? Why are you shouting like that?" Helen asked.

"It's nothing. Let's go back to sleep," I told her.

"You always talk in your sleep and today was no exception," she revealed.

"I do? Maybe I should see a doctor. Don't worry, let's go back to sleep," I said.

It was almost 05:00 and I could not find sleep. Just then, my cell phone started ringing. On the screen I could read 'Paul calling.'

"Hello, good morning.... You are not disturbing at all. I'm up already.... You know I will never deny you anything. Of course I will accompany you to our friend Mr William. I was also planning to go there one of these days.... 07:30 is ok with me.... See you at the bus stop.

I briefed Helen on what I planned to do with my friend later that day and she had no problem with it. I felt really happy that morning following our reconciliation the previous day. We felt like we just met each other and the excitement as well as the dream of spending our lives next to each other were reborn. We wished things could remain that way and never change. But life was not made like that. Changes had to come and a good number of them with trials. We could only wish and wish.

At 07:15 I boarded a taxi for Bamenda Up Station. I got to the premises of Guarantee Express which was the last towards the outskirts of town and located on the right side of the highway that linked Bamenda to other parts of the country at 07:30 and realized Paul was not there yet. I decided to go for a short stroll. So, I got out of the company's premises and decided to walk back towards the direction that led to the city. I could see the other different agencies that relocated there on both sides of the high way. I noticed that many of the travel agencies that obeyed the law were completely empty. There were no signs of life in them as they were covered by grass. However, the decision to relocate there was imposed by the authorities of the city of Bamenda who considered the travel agencies partly responsible for the heavy traffic congestion in the city. But after their relocation to Up Station, the traffic situation in the city did not improve. Instead it worsened, indicating that the cause of the problem laid somewhere else. The reality was that the ever increasing numbers of new or second hand cars that were acquired by residents of the city became disproportionate to the available road network. As a result, some of the travel agencies decided to go back to their initial locations in the heart of the city which made things a lot easier for their customers. That explained why some of the premises were abandoned to grass and stray animals. Whether the authorities were incompetent or lacked foresight or were just pretending to give the population the impression that they were doing something about the traffic problem by asking travel agencies to relocate to Up Station as some critics claimed, was a different story. But one thing was clear and it was that the authorities of the city saw and identified a problem but blamed it on those they were not supposed to. Personally, I saw in their actions a reflection of the way the regime in place viewed and initiated actions which in most cases turned out to be waste of time, energy and resources. That notwithstanding, I decided to head back to Guarantee Travel Agency premises where Paul and I agreed to meet. When I got closer, I could spot him craning his eyes from left to right searching for me. I got to him and glanced at my watch and it was exactly 08:00.

We boarded a Toyota Coaster bus and it headed back in the direction of the city. After descending the station hill, we turned right and headed east, passing through Nkwen which was one of the three villages that was swallowed up by the city. In twenty minutes, we were completely out of the city. Everyone in the bus was quiet and there was music booming from the speakers that hung from the roof of the bus over our heads. Some people were nodding to the rhythm of the music while others took out books and were trying to assimilate one or two things from them.

We had not gone five kilometres when we met a police checkpoint and had to stop. The bus driver did not get out of the bus as most drivers did and parked the bus right in the middle of the road. Two policemen came near the bus. One of them asked to see the documents of the vehicle and the other wanted the passengers to present their national identity cards. He started in front with those who were seated next to the driver. He got to the fourth row where I was and everyone held out his or her identity card except me. He skipped me and checked those of the rest of the passengers and then came back to me.

"Can I see your identification papers," he asked.

"Sure. But I'll like to see yours first," I said.

"Haven't you seen everybody present their Identity cards without complaining?" he asked.

"I am not everybody and will not show you anything without seeing yours", I said.

He stood there by the bus not knowing what to do as there was also a long cue of vehicles that was behind us hooting nonstop. He resorted to threats.

"I will say this just once. Show me your identification papers or get out of the bus," he ordered.

That attracted the attention of one of his colleagues who came to see what was going on. He asked what was wrong and his colleague who just threatened me told him. He asked the colleague who threatened me to calm down and let him handle the situation. His aggressive colleague shifted aside and gave him room to address me.

"Why are you making things difficult?" he asked politely.

"I am not making anything difficult. I just want to see things done the way they are supposed to be done. By way of protocol, when you walk up to somebody, you have to present yourself first. Ask him if he did that. He has no name on his uniform which is an indication that he disobeyed the minister of defence's orders. In addition to that, maybe he does not have a national or professional card on him. Yet, he is insisting that I present my identification papers to him. Who is he? Only last week we saw images on TV of some men who were arrested wearing military and police uniforms passing around as real men in uniform. Up in the Far North, those armed robbers who extort, rape, maim and even kill innocent citizens do wear such uniforms. Can you deny it? Would he have allowed anyone in this bus to go if he /she said that she had forgotten her identity card at home? I don't think so. It would have been an opportunity to make money," I said.

"You've made your point and I understand your worries. My friend used the wrong approach. I'm sorry for that. This is my card," he said brandishing his professional card.

"I removed my professional card from my shirt pocket and handed it to him. He looked at the passport size photograph on it and also looked at me to make sure that it was actually mine.

"So, you are a teacher," he remarked handing my document back to me. "No doubt you were talking too much.

We took off again after wasting seventeen minutes at the check point. Unpredictable as the weather could be, the sun soon gave way to the rain. Inside the bus, my verbal exchange with the men in uniform generated some mixed reactions. There were those who praised me for my courage and others who attacked me for wasting their time. My friend was most critical.

"That big mouth of yours will get you into serious trouble some day. I have told you that several times," he said.

"If I get into trouble after making my point, I won't mind," I told him.

50 kilometres from the police checkpoint, the tar ended. We had to continue on a road not tarred in the heart of the rainy season. The road was wide but very slippery and blessed with many potholes. Such a road was definitely not good for pregnant women. It took us three hours to cover a distance of 25 kilometres to get to Kimton village. The journey by bus had to end there since the road ahead became too narrow. We were forced to alight and board a Land Rover which was the only vehicle capable of covering the remaining16 kilometres to our destination.

We started off at 16:00. That last lap of the journey was the most tedious and nerve wrecking of all. The vehicle got stuck in large potholes full of mud from time to time and we had to get out of the vehicle and push. There was a particular pothole which actually looked like a crater in the middle of the road. Just like the previous ones we confronted earlier, it was full of mud. The front tyres went through but the back tyres got stuck. The pushing became more demanding. Those who stood directly behind the spinning back tyres to push were the most unfortunate and Paul was one of them. He looked like a devil surprised by daylight after one of the tyres splashed a large amount of mud on him. It was not an easy exercise as even women had to lend a helping hand at that stage of the journey. A good number of the passengers were already used to the ordeal and left those of us experiencing it for the first time to wonder why they had to take off their shoes and clothes at some point. Paul and I were not happy and some of the passengers sympathised with us.

"You just have to manage the situation," one of them said.

" Our so called politicians have made several unfulfilled promises and now we are tired of them. Before the last elections they brought some heavy equipment and kept them where the tar ended and promised that they would tar this road if we voted for them. Immediately after the voting exercise, the heavy equipment disappeared over night. They shall be back here when the next elections are around the corner" another passenger lamented.

Everybody sighed and boarded the Land Rover again. It was already 18:00 and we still had three kilometres to go.

"There are no serious potholes again from here and so you will no longer have to go down to push," said the driver once we started off again.

"May God be our helper," Paul said jokingly. "I'm pretty sure that if a man happens to fall in love with a woman from this area and has to go through this cavalry to see her parents, he would change his mind on the way."

That threw the rest of the passengers into laughter. I think they badly needed it after so much tension, effort and frustration.

It was 18:20 when we got to Bibom village. It was not quite dark yet. It seemed that everybody in the village knew Mr William and we were immediately taken to his house. He was in and welcomed us to his home. We badly needed a bath and our good friend knew it well. There was no time to sit and chat with him or his wives and children. We had our bath and off to bed we went after having supper.

8

It was 05:00 when I heard a cock crow. Being very sensitive even when I was in a deep sleep, it chased all sleep from my eyes. The clearness of the crow indicated that it was in the kitchen of William's third wife which was very close to the guest room that we occupied. Unable to find sleep, I just laid in bed wondering what the day in that remote village was going to look like.

At 05:50, the day was already showing its face. Birds were singing outside to indicate that it was day dawn. There was no need for watches in Libom Village as people knew the time listening to cock crow, the singing of birds and the position of the sun. I stepped out and all the surroundings were green. They even got greener as the early morning twilight fell on the whole village. The hills were so inviting that at a second glance it was as if they were beckoning. No nature lover would be strong enough to resist such beauty. The village was highly agricultural as most villages in the region. Most people could be seen going to their farms very early that morning.

Mr William had three wives and fifteen children. They were all busy outside assembling farm tools ready to go to the fields. Each wife had five children. Mr William apportioned lands to each of his wives and their children. Each wife cultivated crops on the land apportioned to her. That was to avoid confrontation and maintain the peace and unity of the family. Peace and unity were the two commodities that were always under attack in most polygamous homes. It was from the farms that the women got food to feed their children and also sold some to educate them. What was sold in the market had to carry the signature of Mr William though most of the time, he did the selling while each wife and her children worked in the fields. In the case where his wives took the produce to the markets, they had to carry every franc back to their husband. He was the head of the family and charged with maintaining peace and order in the family. He had to distribute the resources in the family equally so as to avoid conflict. But being a polygamous home with many children life could sometimes be survival of the fittest. Conflict was unavoidable in such situations and so Mr William, at times, had to run his home with an iron fist.

Mr William's house was in a capital L shape. It was divided into what looked like apartments. They were five in all including one meant only for strangers. Each apartment was made up of three bedrooms and a large sitting room. One room was occupied by the mother of the house while the other two were for her children. Each sitting room was equipped with a 1.5x 2m bamboo cupboard and a single C-shaped couch also made out of bamboo. Mr William's apartment was well equipped with two well made sets of chairs, with one occupying the dining section. A large cupboard made of hard wood and well varnished stood at one end of the sitting room. It accommodated drinks of different sorts, breakable plates, a large TV set and a deck. There were tiles on the floor and a good wool carpet as well. TV images could not be received in that part of country given the enclave nature of the area. There was no electricity there either. Some of the villagers who were a bit well off were able to watch movies with small generators supplying energy. Of course, the well furnished apartment of our friend served as a venue for family meetings and the reception of very important guests. His wives also took their turns there.

It was 06:10 when Mr William's wives and fifteen children left for the fields. Only the three of us were left at home. I was surveying and admiring the surroundings while Paul was still in the guest apartment. I could not tell if he was still asleep or if he was just lying and letting his imagination go wild. Mr William on his part was in his apartment. I couldn't tell what he was thinking or planning to do that day. Whatever the case I decided to go into Mr William's apartment and just then Paul emerged from the guest house. We both went in together and met him sitting on one of the chairs.

"Good morning 'Oga'," we greeted.

"Good morning my friends," he replied. "How was your night?

"It was wonderful. I slept like a king after yesterday's tedious journey," I replied.

"I felt like someone who had received snake beatings. I think all that pushing yesterday is responsible for my being so tired. I don't think I will go anywhere or do anything today. Anyway, I just came to say good morning and find out how your family is doing. I know they must have gone to the farm by now. I'm going back to bed for round two," Paul said and left for the guest house again.

I remained with William in his apartment. I examined everything that my eyes could fall on in the sitting room. I looked at the pictures of him, his wives and fifteen children. He smiled as he saw me looking at them with keen interest.

"You have a lovely family," I said.

"You can say that again, they are my pride," he said with a broad smile.

"It is far too large, don't you think? Why did you decide to have so many children with three wives?" I asked.

"Look Smith, I have a very large estate and need people to work in it. Philomena could not give me those fifteen children and so, I had to get Josephine and Joan to assist her. Besides, when I was only with my first wife, controlling her was a big problem. She had no respect for me. She always wanted me to hear from her. That problem was solved with the coming of the other two wives. As our people say here, 'a woman's cure is just another woman', he said laughing.

"I still maintain that three wives and fifteen children are too large," I insisted.

"Can't you see something and just appreciate it without saying what is wrong with it?" he asked.

"Well, good enough you have mentioned the word 'appreciate'. We cannot appreciate something just by looking at one side of that thing. We have to look at the good side and the bad side and that is when we can comfortably talk of appreciation. At least you should be thankful that you have me here to tell you what is wrong with having such a large family," I said.

"I see nothing wrong with my family. They help me to till the fields and plant crops which we harvest and sell. I use the money to provide for their needs. For instance, when they are sick I take them to the hospital, I feed them, buy clothes and shoes for them and also give them pocket allowance," he explained.

"Is that all?" I asked.

"What else is there? Am I not capable of taking care of my children?" he asked.

"From all the examples you have given, I see you can take care of them indeed. But you have not mentioned one thing; Education. How many of them go to school?" I asked.

"Did you just say education? What are you talking about? Look at my first son, how old is he? He has been to the university, same with my second son and fourth daughter. What have they made of all that education? The certificates they have obtained are getting cold in the cupboard. Maybe you would tell me they are lying fallow. They are back here still expecting me to give them pocket money. Of course, I am their father and know it is my duty to take care of them. But when I spend huge sums of money sending them to school, I expect them to find work after their studies and take care of their younger ones. But look at the situation; they are back here with me after years of education. I therefore see no need wasting money to send the rest of them to school when they will end up here with me," he concluded with a sigh.

"I understand your situation perfectly well. It is the wish of every parent to see their children find a place to earn daily bread after years of education. But have you asked yourself if the type of formal education you gave your children was the right one? By the way, did you send them to a technical, professional, vocational or a grammar school?

"To a grammar School of course! That is where most people send their children. I could not send them to a technical school because people would have mocked me," he said.

"And why did you think people were going to mock you if you sent your children to technical schools?" I asked.

"For the simple reason that such schools are meant for children who are not intelligent enough to cope in grammar schools," he replied.

"There you are! Do you send your child to a particular school because you think it will benefit that child or because you see others sending their children there?" I asked.

81

Mr William became speechless. He took his eyes off me and started staring at the floor. That gave me the chance to go on with my teaching.

"Our corrupt government today cannot employ all the students that our universities send out every year. So, the best schools to send your children are professional, technical, vocational or commercial schools. Students out of such schools do not necessarily have to depend on the government. If your children were from such schools, they would have employed themselves somewhere using the skills acquired from there. Certificates from our grammar universities are just flat certificates because the courses offered in such institutions are not career oriented. With our grammar education, children move from the nursery, secondary through high school to the university and right back to the streets as hawkers and taxi drivers. Do you know what worries me in all that?" I asked.

"No, not until you tell me," William said.

"It is the total indifference of our so called leaders regarding education in this country. Why should they first of all bother? Their children are studying in the best universities in Europe and America all sponsored with the poor tax payer's money. They are here polluting the whole country with grammar schools that do not give adequate training to our children. How many state owned technical secondary and high schools do we have in this country, let alone universities? Just a handful of secondary and high schools. They are good at copying from the West but are unable to copy the career oriented systems of education on which the foundations of such western nations have been built. What a pity!!! Come election time, they will come promising 'new grammar schools' if you vote for them. They open schools not because they feel that there are real social needs for them but for political reasons. For instance, an active member of the ruling party might have been very instrumental in the success of the last elections and to acknowledge his contribution, a grammar school is created and he is made boss of the school. Whether he has the necessary mental and tactical skills to manage a school is not important. What is important is for the party comrade to be compensated. You can see there that the future of the future generation is sacrificed on the altar of greed and mediocrity. How do they expect someone to manage something which has been given to him as a form of compensation? Yet, when they hear the slogan ; 'Education for all', they simply pick up the lyrics and start chanting without asking what type of education their citizens really need. Other countries are developing because they decided at some point to invest in the education of their citizens who were to later on become their work force. No country develops without having a qualified work force. Our confused leaders are talking of making our country an emerging economy by the year 2035. With which work force when they are inviting and appointing foreigners to head some of our companies? Instead of investing in the professional training of the children of this country, they prefer to buy expensive 4x4 vehicles with some costing over eighty million francs to ride in and make us feel how important they are. They have greatly contributed to the negative way people look at technical education in this country. Majority of people believe that technical education is for those who cannot make it in the Grammar Schools and the government keeps backing them in that line of thinking by opening more and more grammar schools which most are unfortunately under-staffed. William look; if a child is in a particular system of education and gets to year four secondary school without being able to use the knowledge acquired practically, then there is something wrong with that system of education. Our leaders have not yet realised this. What they have realised is that they can use the 'education for all' slogan and organise expensive trips to Europe to beg for money which will end up in private bank accounts back in that same Europe," I said.

"Whoop my friend! I thought that your talking habit in our primary school days must have reduced by now. But I can see that it has instead worsened with the passing years. Well, just be careful that it does not land you into trouble some day. You are the ones that have gone far in education and understand these things better," he said.

"I will always remember that," I told him. "Coming back to you, I can't understand why you have sentenced some of your children to a life of chronic illiteracy simply because their elder brothers and sister can't find work after years of education. You really beat my imagination. Look, the fact that your older children can't find work now does not mean they will never find it. No condition is permanent my friend. It is better to have those certificates without work than not to have them and the brain is (be?) equally empty. What kind of a man are you? We are in the computer age and people cannot afford to be intellectually empty. Now, do me a favour by sending those children to technical or vocational schools. The world is changing at the speed of lightening and we have to change with it. I think you should create time and come to the city for some computer lessons."

"Me? Oh no, no way! Formal education is no longer for people like me. I'm too old for that," he said.

He paused for a while in a pensive mood and then went on again.

"No, it is not possible. Remember I left primary school more than twenty years ago and I was far much older than you were then. What do you think I can get into this head after such a long time? That would only be torturing myself. Let's forget about it," he said with disgust.

"And what about your children?" I asked.

"I will think about what you said but I still think that it is a waste of resources. To me, being able to read and write is enough. Look at me for example, I'm a successful man, yet I did not go far in school. What we really need to succeed is common sense and I don't think one can acquire that in school. All left to me, they would end after obtaining their First School Leaving certificates," he said and turned his face.

"I think you are the worst thing that has ever happened to the civilized world. So, all my lecturing has been falling on deaf ears. Just listen to yourself speak. Have you thought of what might happen to your large family if you dropped dead? Are you sure all of them would like to be farmers like you? Please my friend; it is not a matter of considering what I have said. It is a matter of doing what I have said without sitting down to think. It will save your family. You have so much money. Where do you think you can really invest that money other than in your children? If you close your eyes today, your family might descend into chaos; this wife and her children might want to throw out that wife and her children; the strong ones would want to throw out the weak ones; the lazy ones would like to seize all lands and sell and you think of the rest. Is that the legacy you want to leave behind? Think about it," I said and walked out of his apartment.

9

It was almost midday and I started feeling bumpy. I needed some sprinkling to get back on form. I walked back to the guest apartment and there was dead silence. I think Paul was still asleep. I took water in a bathing bucket and moved to the modern toilet in the guest apartment. I emerged after 15 minutes and saw Paul walking outside. He decided to have a shower too. We both moved to Mr William's apartment after that. We wanted to watch a movie and Mr William went and turned on the generator. The movie we watched was 'Endless Tomorrow' which was a local movie depicting the frustration of a young graduate who could not find work after school. That movie provoked a lot of noise from Mr William.

"You see the stress our system of education and society as a whole put on our children?" he asked.

There was no response from Paul or myself. We concentrated on the movie. More noise came when an employer asked Stephanie, the protagonist to sleep with him before she got the job she was looking for. She refused and went on to pick up a job with a foreign company which implanted itself in the country towards the end of the movie. When the movie ended I was itchy to make my last point on education to Mr William.

"You are quick to see the hurdles that girl in the movie goes through to find a job and you condemn education in its entirety. But you seem to forget the end. The fact that she finds a job at the end of the movie confirms what I have been hammering in your head all day, that no condition is permanent. Please send them to school and let them get their certificates. Even if they do not get jobs, they would, at least, have knowledge. But if you do not want to send them to school, send some of them out of here to go and experience life elsewhere like the city. That common sense you talked about so much could work if they are in the city even if they do not go far in school," I said.

It was unfortunate that the movie portrayed male nationals as those that tried to sexually exploit young girls who went to them for jobs. It was painful but it was the hard reality. Foreigners on the other hand were presented as those who upheld meritocracy as the protagonist found work after her documents were examined. There can be no meritocracy in situations where sex is involved. That was one of the things that made our friend unwilling to send his children to school, especially the female children. But I capitalised on what he said about thinking of sending his children to school.

It was 15:00 when the movie ended and William suggested that we watch another one to end the day. Paul and I wanted to go and explore the village which was sparsely populated. Mr William's immediate neighbour was some 100 hundred meters away. They were separated by cultivated farms. That was a reflection of the settlement around there. The roads were well made though not tarred with well carved outside gutters. We gathered from the villagers on our tour that it was thanks to community work that they had roads. With the pathetic nature of the only road that connected them to the rest of the outside world, the inhabitants wondered if the government knew they existed. Maintaining the village road was not much of an issue since only Mr William owned a Toyota Hilux. The other villagers either owned motor-bikes or bicycles which were considered signs of wealth. The village landscape was green with maize planted here and there. That indicated that the village, just as many others around, was mainly agricultural. The villagers were very hospitable. Some curious ones asked us about life in the city while others wanted us to confirm or refute what they had heard about strange happenings in the city. We tried to provide answers as best as we could and those that listened left feeling satisfied. There was food in abundance in every house we visited. Of course we could not eat everywhere we went and that disappointed some of our newly made friends.

It was 17:30 when we decided to end our tour and return home. William's three wives and children were at home when we got there. Each wife had to take a bath and then enter the kitchen to cook the family evening meal. Each of them had to bring their husband's share as well as that for the guests in a special dish. William had to eat at least one-quarter of what each woman brought. Failure to do so was definitely going to signal the beginning of trouble as they stood there to see him eat their food and judge from his expression whether the food was good or not. That was another downside of being a polygamist. I honestly did not want to imagine myself in his place even for a second. Sometimes, stomach disorders were inevitable as the women brought in different varieties of food which sometimes could not be mixed like on the evening of our arrival. He spent the whole night alternating between his bedroom and the toilet after consuming everything his three wives brought.

"I don't know if these women sometimes team up to kill me," he told Paul and me the next morning. Whatever the case, he was condemned to go through the ordeal if he did not want trouble. It was a price to pay for being a polygamist and I seized the opportunity to mock him when he complained. However, we had our supper with our friend's three wives watching. We ate with a lot of appetite which made them happy. When we were through, they thanked us for eating their food and cleared the used dishes. We remained in our friend's sitting room chatting while waiting for bed time. It came at 20:00. We separated and retired to our various rooms.

The next morning, the second day after our arrival in the village, I woke up at 09:00. The sun was not shinning and the sky was getting cloudy. From every indication it was going to rain. I realized that everybody was at home. They decided to take that day off to take care of things at home. Even Paul woke up early. Mr William proposed that we go to one of his farms, which was some 3 kilometres away, to tap palm wine. Paul and I eagerly accepted. He then advised us to put on clothes which covered our whole body as the place was infested not only with mosquitoes but with tsetse flies as well. Since the sky was unpredictable, we decided to go with the car. It started drizzling shortly after we left the house.

It took us no time to cover the 3 kilometre distance that separated us from the farm. We soon got to a point where the car could not go any further because the road became too narrow. We had to leave the car and complete the remaining 200 meters ahead of us on foot before taking a bend that plunged down a valley to the farm. The slope was really steep.

"You can go to your school to any level but you will always come back to us for pocket money," William said with a certain air of arrogance, handing his calabash to me and his cutlass and tapping knife to Paul. He pocketed his hands as we went along. The drizzling had just given way but the sun was still to show its face. We got to the bend descending to the farm and William still had his hands in his pocket. He wore canvas shoes which were very slippery even on level ground. It was worse when fungus covered the surface. I think he forgot that it just drizzled and since no water could be seen on the ground with the naked eye, he tended to neglect precaution. I did not remind him though I anticipated what could happen if we started descending with him while his hands were still in his pocket. Maybe I really wanted him to fall. I hated him for his arrogance and conservative thinking. If he had been a kid, I would have taken a whip and whooped his butt. I did not know what Paul was thinking or whether he also anticipated what was going to happen to our friend. But William had to lead the way since Paul and I were going to the farm for the first time. I was the first from behind. We had hardly started descending when William slipped and landed on his back. He succeeded in raising his head and taking his hands out of his pocket but fell to the bottom of the steep slope on his buttocks. He was brutally stopped by a bunch of bamboo sticks which someone laid across the footpath that led to the farm at the bottom of the slope. He was lucky that there were no stones along the path. Paul and I ran after him calling and feeling very worried. We got to him and found him on his feet struggling to get the layers of mud he had gathered on his brutal descend off his trousers.

"Are you alright?" Paul and I asked simultaneously.

William did not respond. He continued removing the mud from his trousers without daring to look at us in the face. With no answer coming from William, we stood there watching him in silence.

"Are you guys asking that question from the bottom of your hearts?" he asked without looking at us at last.

Paul and I glanced at each other and did not answer him because our necks were already swollen with laughter.

"Anyway, the down fall of a man is not the end of his life," he said gesturing and continued on his path. Paul and I could not hold it anymore and exploded with laughter. William, who was a few meters (be consistent with your British English or American English: meters or metres) ahead of us, stopped and stared at us. He sat down and joined us in the laughter.

"I knew you too were dying of laughter when we met you by that bunch of bamboo. That's why you did not want to look at us and pretended to be angry," Paul told William.

We still had some 300 meters to go before getting to the section of the palm bush that belonged to our friend. He led the way and since we were no longer on a sloppy surface, there was no fear of falling. We moved from one cluster of bamboo trees to the other collecting small calabashes and emptying their contents in a ten litre calabash that we carried there from home. We could not go round the whole farm because the big calabash got full. It was exactly 13:30 when we finished and we decided to go back home.

We left the farm and were about to ascend the steep hill that led to where the car was parked when we heard someone shouting in a very loud voice. It was a male voice and was coming in the direction of the farm we just left. William recognised the voice as that of his neighbour. We left the palm wine and tapping instruments by the side of the foot path and rushed to the direction of the voice. It took us 10 minutes to get there and we found a man struggling to run for his dear life. At first glance, one would have thought that he was running away from a ghost. When he saw us running towards him, he fell to the ground. I think he certainly ran out of energy.

"Mr. Simon, what is it? Who is chasing you? William asked worried just as we were.

"I...I...I....I've ssssssseen a....a...a....a....a...sssssssss," he stammered and passed out.

We did not know the name of a thing or animal whose name began with 's' which he was trying to flee from. But that did not matter then. Getting him out to safety was more important. I took off my jacket and handed it to William who used it to fan him while Paul and I carried him. Carrying Mr. Simon was not an easy exercise. His bulky size demanded much effort from us. It took us 25 minutes to get to where we kept the calabash of palm wine and tapping instruments. Carrying him while ascending the little hill and then for another 200 meters to get to the car was an uphill task. Since William was bulky too, we proposed that he carried his neighbour to where the land was level and we would take over from there. He agreed and carried Mr. Simon on his back. Midway before we got to level land, it seemed William was running out of steam. Paul and I suggested that he stood still to regain some energy but he refused saying that he would rest when we hit the level land. After moving a few steps further, he started breathing heavily. Then we heard a heavy sound come out from between his legs. The sound was so loud that I thought it was going to cause damage to his trousers. The air became unpleasant and Paul and I who were moving behind him became uncomfortable. Thank God, a little breeze started blowing just then and helped to dispel the unpleasant odour.

He finally made it to level land and Mr. Simon regained consciousness. We held him and helped him to the car. We did not want to start bothering him with questions. So, we just let him be till we got to our friend's house. William did not want to drive his neighbour straight to his own house without being certain that he was going to be ok or taken care of by his family if at all he was in some kind of health crisis. For that reason we led Mr. Simon into the sitting room of William's second wife's apartment. There, he was made to sit on the c-shaped bamboo couch. I sat next to him while my two friends went out. William soon returned with a mug of water for Simon to drink. Mr. Simon drunk a good amount and was looking revitalized again. But he was not allowed to go without eating and drinking something. So, he was asked to stay put.

You might be wondering why our friend did not take Mr. Simon to his apartment but to that of his second wife. Well, the truth was that his attire was really dirty and nasty. The nastiness was further compounded by some mud he fell in while he was trying to run away from I don't know what. If he was in the city looking like that, he would have been mistaken for a madman.

That notwithstanding, William who left after giving his neighbour a mug of water soon returned with his second wife following him closely behind. They were in some kind of queue. William had a plate of rice and stew alongside a big fish in his hands while his second wife held a jar of water. They all wore smiles on their faces as they were coming to entertain our patient. But just when William extended the plate to our patient who stretched his arms to receive it, something unusual happened. All of a sudden, Simon sprang to his feet, gathered William and his second wife and pushed them for some two meters before they all crashed to the ground outside in the yard. I wondered what on earth provoked that kind of reaction. Any other person would have first ran out to help William and his wife to their feet but I did not do that. I instead sought to know what must have been so frightful to have ejected Mr. Simon from his seat. It was then I saw the tail of Minou, the cat of the house, swinging like the arm of a pendulum from left to right from under the bamboo couch our patient sat on. That tail would not have been swinging like that for no reason. From every indication, Minou just finished eating a sumptuous catch. It then dawned t that what scared Mr. Simon to death at the farm might have been a snake. Minou's swinging tail merely helped to enlarge a fresh wound.

Outside, there was more drama. William exclaimed to the top his voice to vent out his anger and frustration after Paul came and helped him off the ground. That attracted the attention of some curious neighbours and other village passer-bys.

"What is it Mr. William? Your voice could be heard right from the road. What is happening?" one of them asked.

"Is it not Mr. Simon?" William responded in anger.

"What about Mr. Simon? What has happened to him?" asked another.

"Ask him! There he is. He can better answer your questions," William said.

"Mr. Simon, what is happening to you?" the strangers asked him.

"I saw something black sweeping the ground from left to right from under that chair," he explained pointing to the chair. "It reminded me of the very big snake I saw today at the farm. I was afraid it might swallow me if I was unable to get away quickly,"

The explanation drew a lot of sympathy from the villagers. He was brought a chair outside and made to sit down. Mr William's second wife brought him another plate of rice. He ate and regained full possession of himself. He was then taken to his house by the passersby who streamed into William's compound. One of William's daughters gathered the spilled rice on the ground with a broom. I decided to go and have a bath just as Paul did. We gathered in William's apartment after bathing and drank the palm wine we got from the farm. I got drunk after gulping a few glasses and moved directly to my room. I woke up at 20:00 feeling very hungry and moved to William's sitting room. Luckily for me he was still awake watching a movie. Paul was sitting on one of the chairs but was dead asleep. I think the palm wine also took a toll on him. I walked straight to the dining table and dished a plate of rice and stew with which I filled my stomach. William proposed a glass of palm wine to push down the rice. I turned down the offer because I knew that palm wine and rice could be a very dangerous combination especially at night. However, I shook Paul to get up and go to bed but he too went immediately to the dining table instead. He ate foufou corn made out of corn flour and okra soup before leaving for his room. I also left for my room after wishing William a goodnight.

10

I got out of my room the next morning at 08:00. No one could be seen around the house except Paul. Everyone had gone to the farm including William. Paul and I wondered what we could do given that it was our third day in the village. I proposed that we go visit the local Government Primary School to see how they were doing. He approved of my idea and we went into our rooms to change clothes and left.

We got to the school after some 25 minutes of serious trekking. The infrastructure was built using local materials. The buildings had mud earth walls and thatched roofs. From what we observed, the thatched roofs badly needed replacement because the classrooms become flooded each time it rained. Besides, the floors were not cemented which made them very muddy. The doors of the school were labelled class 1-6. The school was understaffed with classes 2 and 3 having no teachers. In addition, the villagers were poor and could not afford to buy prescribed textbooks. With an average of 40 pupils per class with only the teacher having a text book, the teaching job became too difficult. Consequently it was difficult for the students to do homework. Those were some of the problems we got from our discussion with the class four teacher who saw us and came out to see if he could be of any help to us. Mr. Jonathan was his name and he was pleased to learn that I was a teacher though I did my teaching at the secondary school level. I asked him why he was teaching instead of enjoying his holiday.

"With the lack of textbook and the seeming lack of interest on the part of the pupils, we have to put in a lot of effort. I am trying to introduce the children here to what they would be reading when schools finally reopen. We believe that if they are reading something for the second time, it would better stick in their minds. Teaching in a village like this one is really hell, I must say," he confessed.

What he told us was in sharp contrast to what obtained in the city. Parents there were more enlightened and understood the importance of textbooks in the teaching and learning process. Consequently they bought quite a good number of the textbooks that were absolutely necessary especially for subjects like mathematics, literature, English language and the French language. At least it was better than in the villages where parents considered the payment of fees as the most important thing and the buying of textbooks as a waste of resources. But for teachers in the city to sacrifice their holiday to teach students for free was out of the question. Teaching was done only during official school periods and any extra periods had to be paid for either by the school or the parents. Besides, the classrooms in the city were like jungles. Survival of the fittest was the rule. With the exceptionally large sizes of the classes, slow learners could not really be attended to. I admired Jonathan for the sacrifices he was making for the sake of his pupils as he wanted them to at least measure up to their mates in the towns and cities.

Paul and I decided to go into the classroom to watch Jonathan deliver his lesson. The subject we could see on the chalkboard was domestic science. In order not to distract the pupils, we moved to the back of the muddy classroom.

"Who can name two domestic animals?" he asked.

One pupil raised her hand. "Yes Karen, what is the answer?" the teacher asked.

"Cat," said Karen.

"That is just one and I asked for two," the teacher reiterated. But no hand went up. Even when he called some pupils by name to answer, they did not make any attempt. The teacher looked disappointed and walked out of the classroom. I followed him to see what he was going to do. He went to a cypress tree and deprived it of some of its branches.

"I thought the government made it illegal to use canes in schools," I told him.

"The government is wrong. These children here cannot learn without a cane. They spend their time speaking their mother tongue even in the classroom. We tried to implement the law here but these children developed wings. They refused to do my assignments which I spent my time copying on the board. Even now they do them only when they sense that I might use the cane. When those government official sit in air conditioned offices, they think that all is rosy down here," he said moving hastily back to the class.

I slowed him down by telling him that if the children spent most of their time speaking their mother tongue that was not supposed to be considered a problem. He was supposed to use the pupils' mother tongue if he was from that village to teach them. He admitted that what I said was true but insisted the pupils were going to write official exams in the English language and not their mother tongue. For that reason he had to be strict in preventing the use of the mother tongue in the school milieu. We soon got back to the classroom.

"I will give you two strokes each if you do not provide me with the answers I need," the teacher threatened.

The pupils did not seem bothered at all. It would appear they were more comfortable with receiving the strokes than frying their brains searching for answer their teacher wanted. Only one pupil looked terrified and it was Karen who gave the first answer. I don't think she was ever used to the cane. But I was sure that she was going to be exempted if their teacher decided to punish the class. I could tell where the problem was. It was with the word 'domestic' though there were other possible contributory factors. Maybe some of the pupils knew the answers but were too shy to speak out. Their teacher soon dropped the cane and went on to give a synonym of the word 'domestic' in their mother tongue. Immediately he did that so many hands shot up and he got more answers than he expected. He soon ended the subject and was about to move to the next when Paul and I left the classroom and headed towards the head master's office. The window of his office was open but he was not in. We suspected that with the shortage of staff in the school, he must have gone into one of the classrooms to teach. We then decided to go home.

On our way back, Paul started getting worried about his family especially his pregnant wife who was just a few weeks away from giving birth.

"I want to go back tomorrow. Leaving my wife with the baby sitter and the two kids all alone and staying here too long is not a good idea," he told me. We planned to inform William of our decision that evening and to leave the next morning.

Later that evening, we informed William about our eminent departure the next morning. He was not pleased that we had spent only three days with him. He would have loved to keep us much longer. But being a family man, he

100

understood our situation and had no option but to ask some of his children to prepare some bags of food items for us. His wives thanked us for coming to visit them and promised to make a stopover whenever they made a trip to the city.

Early that Friday morning we boarded one of the five Land Rovers that plied the village road. William jumped in too to see us off two kilometres out of the village. The distance was covered in no time and we parted ways.

"Greet our wives when you get back. I will come to the city at the end of next month. When I come, we shall paint the town red," he said and alighted. The remaining 14 kilometres to where we had to board a bus was less tedious. We descended more than we ascended and it took us less time to cover the distance. We got to Kimton Village and boarded a bus bound for the City of Bamenda.

It was 13:13 when we hit the tar again and it was exactly 55 kilometres to Bamenda Town. We began receiving radio signals again. It was news time on The Silent Voices, FM 94, a private owned radio station. The bus was quiet and even mothers with crying babies were yelled at to make them stop by all possible means. Everyone wanted to get the latest news on what was going on in the city, country and the world at large after being cut off for a while. The volume was increased so that those at the back of the bus could hear the news as well. The presenter started with what made news in and around the city of Bamenda. There was nothing really striking but when he moved to what made news out of the province, we had more than enough to feed our ears on. The most shocking news was a human interest story about a man who was raped at his residence and Fried Stanley, their reporter in Yaounde picked up the story.

"Mr Ngongang is a civil servant working in the governor's office here in Yaoundé," he began. He gets up very early to brave the early morning cold and heavy traffic congestion to be at work at 7:30 and return at 16:30 every working day. He works very hard to provide for his family. Life was good for him or so it seemed until yesterday evening when his troubles started. He returned home from work at 16:30 as usual and made a stopover at a local restaurant to have his evening meal since his wife and two daughters had left for the village to spend some time with an uncle two days earlier. He entered his house at 19:00 and had a good shower. After that he returned to his sitting room to spend some time in front of his TV screen before going to bed. It was then that some four men of the underworld erupted in his house. They wanted money. Mr Ngongang had 20.000 Frs. with him and offered it to them. They were not happy with the amount and started manhandling him. He pleaded with them to accept a cheque of 250.000 Frs. But they still would not accept it. The bad guys considered that the cheque was an easy trick to lure them into a police drag net. Instead they decided to rape him in turns and at the end of it all they took his cell phone and his computer and TV sets. Fortunately for Mr. Ngongang, a neighbour stopped by early this morning to pay a debt which she owed him and found him on the floor naked and bleeding. She immediately alerted the police who arrived some 15 minutes later and began investigations. We only hope they are going to come up with positive results this time around. Mr Ngongang was rushed to the hospital and from what we gathered when we got there, he is presently receiving treatment in the intensive care unit of the Yaoundé General Hospital…."

What came after that report was not of interest to anybody in the bus. The rape of a man and not a woman was just overwhelming and reactions were immediate and varied.

"Heeeeeyyyyyy!" exclaimed one male passenger who was seated at the back of the bus with his hands up as if imploring for divine intervention. "Where is the world heading to? I have been hearing of two men or two women making love to each other only on TV in Europe and the Americas. Has it already come to Africa and right to my own back yard? Cheeeeey! God forbid!"

"My brother, please hold your breath," said another passenger. "So long as you are breathing this air, surprises shall keep springing up. What you need is to develop a strong spirit to be able to absorb some of the shocks which some surprises might bring especially in this 21st century. If you do not, you'd be knocked off your feet someday and you'd wake up only in the world beyond. I even hear that South Africa has already legalised it."

"Heeeeeeeey!!!" the male passenger at the back of the bus continued his wailing. "What is really happening? At first when those men came to your house you would be afraid of your wife and daughters being raped. But now, even you the man are not safe. I can't believe what I'm hearing with these ears."

That news item provoked a storm in the bus. I could read anger and frustration on every face. Some people blamed the high rate of unemployment and the government's inability to create jobs for the insecurity. Others blamed mismanagement and embezzlement of state funds by top ranking government officials for the mess the country found itself in. I did not offer a word. I just listened to the men and women traveller's voice out their frustrations. But despite all they said, one

103

thing was unavoidable and it was change. People found it hard accepting it especially when it came very abruptly. In a nutshell, people were still to realize that the only thing that made us different from other animals was our ability to think and speak. Such actions could no longer be shocking to some of us who went far in education as we leant more about human psychology in the course of our training. As it stood, the news was too overwhelming for so many. As a consequence, the rest of the journey became very solemn and they earnestly longed for it to come to an end soon. I used the short moment to do a lot of thinking on the topic. I wondered what people were going to do if the government in a not too distant future decided to legalise it. Even if it opted not to legalise it but to fight it, how effective could the fight be? Was it going to be policing everyone in their bedrooms? True, homosexuality went against the divine law especially as procreation was concerned. But since people could not be followed to their bedrooms and could not be combated effectively, why not allow things to stay the way they were? I was convinced the problem of child adoption was going to come up sooner or later in the countries where homosexuality was already legalised. But what kind of society would be built out of a future generation raised by homosexuals. It was clear that a homosexual couple could never bear children in my mind and I therefore saw no reason why they should ever clamour for the right to adopt children if the issue came up.

We got back to the city sooner than I had expected. The bus stopped at Total Nkwen and we all alighted. I took just a few steps from the bus when I heard someone calling my name. I turned and saw that it was my old friend Samson and walked up to him.

"Hi Smith, I have not seen you for over a month now and I've just seen you come out of that bus. Were you on a trip?" he asked.

"Yes I was. I went to visit a friend," I told him looking curiously at his face. I saw that there were scars on the right side of his jaw.

"Hey! What happened to you? Did you pick a quarrel with mother crocodile?" I asked

"I fell from a motor-bike. You know how reckless these bike riders in town are. I was very lucky it was not on tar. If it was, the story would have been different now," he replied.

"So, what are you doing here or where are you going to?" I asked.

"I'm going to the port city of Douala to look for a job. I'm hoping that my fortunes might turn around there and I will pick up a job. I don't want my family to keep considering me as a failure. The humiliation is just too much," he said.

"God will surely make a way. Well, good luck and have a nice trip. Please do keep in touch," I said.

"I sure will," he said and left.

In the meantime, Paul had found a taxi and had our luggage loaded in the booth. Since I had nothing so pressing to do at my own house, I decided to go with him to his house to see how his wife was doing. I also called Helen to let her know that I was back in the city.

11

We entered Paul's house at 15:40. His wife was not in the sitting room. Only her two kids and their baby sitter were there watching TV. The children ran and embraced their father and I just watched with a watered mouth. I longed for the day I was going to have children of my own. My friend hugged and kissed his children as if he really wanted to provoke me. Well, I took it as a challenge and planned on normalizing things with Helen's parents as soon as possible. I was not growing any younger and having children late was not good. I thought that it was better to have them while I was still young so that I could watch them grow.

Paul's wife soon emerged from the room. I think she heard us talking in the sitting room and wanted to come and welcome us.

"Welcome back to you both," she said and sank on a chair. "I thought you were never going to come back."

"Well, you can see that we have come back. I could not spend another night knowing full well that you are just days away from giving birth," Paul said.

My friend's wife looked really tired. She had a lot of difficulties carrying herself around. Just leaving their bedroom to join us in the sitting room was a task. I just couldn't help feeling sorry for her and asked her not to ever let my friend put her in that condition again. Her face lit up with a smile when I said that and she asked how our trip was.

"If you can see us here body and soul, it means that the journey was wonderful," I said.

"And you, how has it been in our absence?" Paul asked.

"All has been well oooh! We thank God," she replied.

I decided to come with Paul to his house because I wanted to know how his wife was doing. Since the conclusion after seeing her was that she was fine, I became itchy to get to my own house. I told her and Paul that I would be going home but he protested saying that I could spend the night at his house and go, instead, the next day. I had a choice to make but could not help feeling that if I were married, he wouldn't have been making such a request.

"What about Helen?" I asked.

"Helen will be fine. If she can wait for three days, then just one more night will not kill her. So, just chill my friend," he said.

The look on his wife's face confirmed his wish. She too did not want me to go. She was very happy each time Paul and I were together because our discussions made her laugh. I went to the bathroom first to wash down the yoke of tiredness and regain my freshness. I soon emerged and got into the room Paul said I could spend the night in and put on just simple clothes since I had no intention of going out that evening. On returning to the sitting room, I saw Erica, the friend of Paul's wife. She sat on one of the chairs. Her elbows rested on her lap with her hands supporting her head. From her posture, even a blind man could tell that all was not well.

"Did someone seize your boy friend?" I asked.

"Look at your big mouth. I don't blame you," she said laughing. "So you think only boyfriends can make someone unhappy? What are we doing with them anyway?

"Now let's keep jokes aside. What must be eating you up?" I asked.

She sighed and looked at me but did not answer immediately. She took her eyes off me and started staring at the floor with her head still buried in her palms. I sat waiting for an answer. After a few minutes she spoke.

"It is my future mother-in-law. She is insisting that I get pregnant or have a child before her son gets married to me. She claims that we young girls of today cannot be trusted and adds that she would not want a situation where her son has to start spending money moving from one hospital or medical facility to the next because he is looking for a child. More so, she also says that with the high rate of abortion nowadays, getting pregnant before marriage is the only way to ensure that her generation is not lost along the way," she explained.

"Is that what is making you lose appetite?" I asked.

"Smith you don't understand. What if her son gets me pregnant and says that he is not the father and decides not to marry me? Will his mother force me on him? I learned he has three children with different mothers whom he has refused to recognise. What proves that he will not do to me what he did with the other women?" she asked.

"And what is the opinion of her son?" I asked.

"He has the same standpoint as his mother," she replied.

"If he has three children and has refused to recognise them and his mother is scared that her generation might get lost along the way, she could go in for DNA tests to see if they are her grand children. That way, if you are unable to have children with her son, he could go and bring them in and you raise them as your own. That is only if the mothers are ready to part with their children. They too have rights over their children. But if you really want my humble opinion, I think you should drop that guy like a hot potato and ask him to go and get married to his mother. A man who cannot make decisions that affect his own life independently is not a man and cannot run a home. How can he allow his mother to be making decisions in his own house? Is it normal? Decisions in your home must be made by you and your husband and not mothers-in-law or fathers-in-law. Go for someone who will respect you and your wishes and not give in to the whims and caprices of his mother," I told her.

"Thank you for your advice. I will reflect over what you have said and decide what to do," she said.

I don't think Paul's wife approved of what I said from the expression on her face. I guess she had a contrary view or agreed just partially to what I said. She had always known me to be a radical who was sometimes in her view 'too severe'. I knew I always spoke my mind and stood firm to defend what I knew was right. But I had never succeeded in establishing the link between objectivity and radicalism which Paul's wife always tried to subject me to. Her friend's face brightened up after I spoke to her and she said goodbye to her friend and left. Paul's wife looked at me, smiled and shook her head as if to say 'you will never change'.

We spent the whole evening watching TV, until 21:00 when Paul's wife decided to retire to their bedroom. Her babysitter and two-year old son went to bed much earlier. Paul and I remained in the sitting room. We had all our attention focused on a cow boy movie that was playing on the Action channel and we made comments about it. He soon diverted my attention from the movie to what I intended to be in the distant future.

"Would you like to move up the social ladder or would like to remain a classroom teacher?" he asked.

"Everybody dreams of getting up the social ladder within the field he or she finds herself in after putting in a good number of years. Every society that is normal and governed properly functions like that. But posts are commercialised

110

these days. As a result, former students come to lord over those that taught them in schools. Things in this country are really turning up side down," I said.

"I was asking because I have connections with those that manage affairs in the ministry of education. They are selling the posts of discipline masters, vice principals and principals. What you need is between 250,000 francs to half a million to get the one you want," he said.

"Look my friend, even if I have the money, I would never buy a post. My longevity in service and competence are supposed to be the only tools my superiors are supposed to use in deciding whether I should be promoted or not. Money is not supposed to come into it. Those who go and buy their promotions with money are those who are incompetent and will make the country stagnant or slide backward," I said.

"Well, we can only condemn but there is nothing we can do. Many people are using it to get up the social ladder. They do it only for the financial benefits that come with promotion and nothing else. Ask some of those who have become bosses using money to perform a certain task and they will shamelessly tell you that they can't do it. That is the path this country has taken and many people are using it to better their situations. This is a country where today you are somebody and tomorrow you might be nobody because there is no career profile for public sector workers. Can you really blame people for doing things the way they are doing them? The classrooms have chronic shortage of teachers because through bribes a good number of them are taken out and made administrators. In some schools, the newly appointed administrators do not have offices and they just go to the schools they are sent, to loiter while waiting for the end of the month. At the end, there is more money spent and virtually no work done. If the trend continues, I'm sure in the future, we will see schools where administrators outnumber the teaching staff. Since you are not prepared to play the game, be ready to see one of your former students come and lord over you. Bribery and corruption has engulfed every sector of this economy and the situation in your ministry of education seems to be the most alarming. Look at the teachers' training colleges. They are filled with wives of businessmen and rich public sector workers. Competitive entrance exams into such schools are organised each year but they have remained largely for formality. A name that gets on the final list of those admitted into the institutions is the one that has paid a huge amount of money. Getting a registration or matriculation number in the public service seems to be more important than actually going there because service to the community is a call. Otherwise, why would someone who has graduated from the second cycle teacher's training college shy away from examination classes or a high school under the pretext that she cannot handle it?" Paul asked.

"I guess corruption creates room for half baked scholars and people who are incompetent to get to places or occupy posts they could never dream of occupying in their life time. A country with such people at the helm can only head towards disaster. What kind of material do you want someone with a little brain to produce. He or she will produce only something that reflects his or her brain level. Such a person could be a danger to children entrusted into his or her care," I said.

"I agree with you. Someone told me that the development level of any country is a reflection of the educational level of its ruling class. Really, look at most of those heading a good number of our primary as well as some of the secondary and high schools in the towns and cities. They are mostly women who happen to be the wives of businessmen or relatives of those who make decisions. Some might be quick to say that those who govern attach a lot of importance to female empowerment and that is why women are appointed to posts of responsibility but the bottom line is that those appointments hide a lot of corruption underneath. Such corruption can only bring falling standards of education or education that will be of no use to the learners when they leave school," he said.

"If you know that trading of posts is helping to destroy this country, why do you want to connect me to those who are destroying it?" I asked.

"Who does not like to have a good life? If that is the only way to get it, why not take it? People who really love to see things done in the right way are unfortunately in a terrible minority. What can we really do to turn things around? At the start of each new academic year, credits are given to run schools. The credits are deducted by those people who the money has to go through and what the principal receives to use in running a whole school is very little. Out of the little he finally receives, he has to set aside an amount that he will give to any of his superiors who might want to visit his school in the course of the academic year whereas, there might be classrooms without chalk or black to darken the chalkboard. Those same superiors have displacement allowances but still will not allow the little that is allocated to run the schools. That aside, when one of their exceptional big bosses has to leave the capital to visit the region or province, the principals are asked to make contributions to receive him or her. Such contributions still have to come only from the credits that are given to them to run their schools. If the principals do not do that, they might be removed from their posts. You might be surprised that you are the teacher but I'm the one telling you what goes on in schools. I know because a good number of those principals are my friends and we often talk of the rubbish that goes on in this country. At the end of the day, what is a school judging from the context of this country? They are institutions where hard working party militants are given posts as compensation, a place where big bosses come and get their money for petrol, an institution which is not really out to arm the students or learners physically and mentally for the job market but to keep them from rioting because of joblessness and disturbing the peace of those in power. In this country right now, the ministry of education is the most corrupt, the most disorganised and the ministry which has the most uneducated people. That might sound ironic but it might interest you to know that the worst human right violations take place in human right institutions," he said.

I was dumbfounded and did not know what to say. I only sighed and he sighed as well. He remained pensive for a short while and then opened his mouth to narrate a personal experience he had on one of his business trips.

"Last two months I was travelling to Yaoundé to go and buy some items in a certain company there. It was on a Wednesday and I left the house very early in the morning for Patience Travel Agency where I booked my trip. The bus I had to travel in had to contain seventy passengers and when it was full, everyone on board was asked to come and identify their luggage to make sure that they were loaded in the booth of the bus. One of the pieces of luggage that I saw being loaded in was a big healthy pig. I thought the owner was taking it to Yaoundé to sell at a higher price. There was nothing wrong with that. We soon got to Makene which is midway between Bamenda and Yaoundé and the bus grinned to a halt for the passengers to relax or pick up one or two things before continuing our journey. When we were about to board the bus again, the bus conductor decided to go and check on the animals some people had as luggage. All the passengers were already seated when the bus conductor came in to announce that the big healthy pig was dead. It was then we knew the owner of the pig who happened to have been the principal of one of our big government high schools here in town. He could not control himself and just started shouting at the bus driver and the bus conductor for negligence. He said a lot of things and one of them was that the bus driver and the bus conductor wanted him to be removed from his post. He did not continue the journey with us but alighted there and boarded another bus which was coming to Bamenda from Yaoundé. You know me and my curiosity. I wanted to know why the principal was the one taking a pig to Yaoundé. So I went to the person he sat next to on the bus since I saw them conversing all the time during the course of the journey and asked him if the principal was a pork trader. He told me that his friend wanted to go and see someone in the ministry in Yaoundé who had the power to decide his fate. He wanted to go and bribe those who matter with the pig so that he would not be transferred from the big school he was controlling because there was a lot of money to be managed in that school. That explained everything and proved that the principal was not a pork dealer. If he was, he would have taken the dead pig to Yaoundé, slaughtered it and sold it as if he was the one who killed it," he explained.

"How do you know he would have slaughtered a dead pig to sell to people if he was a pork dealer?" I asked.

115

"I am a businessman and sometimes losses are too painful. That is why some of us sometimes behave as people who have no souls. That is why it is often said that sentiments and business don't go together. Going back to that issue of corruption, I'm sure you can still remember someone who was appointed Regional Delegate of Education for the North West in the morning and he decided to have a party to celebrate his appointment. But in the afternoon of that same day when the appointment party was still going on, a ministerial arête was read at 17:00 appointing someone else to that same post. What in your opinion would have happened to eject someone who had not sat on the chair in his new office even for five minutes? Rumour went round that the second person who was appointed to that same post offered something substantial as bribe for that to happen," he said.

"I can still remember that incident but I've never heard that second part on a substantial bribe being given. Did the rumour mongers say what the huge bribe was?" I asked.

"Well, rumour had it that the substantial bribe was a very healthy cow," he replied. "I was shocked when I heard that. Well, that is the power of corruption. I've not even told you what happened in the plane when I was returning from Europe. You know that I am a very jovial man and like to keep people around me funky. I started a conversation which drew the attention of some people around me who happened to be tourists. We conversed and they really took interest in me and wanted to know where I came from. I told them that I was an African. It seemed back there in Europe that they had lived in neighbourhoods where Africans lived. They had only nice things to say about the Africans. They said how honest, sociable, hard working and loving they were. But one of them insisted on knowing exactly where I came from in Africa. Immediately I mentioned the name of this country, the mood changed. Anyone who had anything valuable around grabbed it and held it tight against his or her chest. The conversation ended and the silence of a graveyard took over until we touched down at the Douala International Airport and separated. Because of the numerous world most corrupt country trophies we have already grabbed, we are looked upon with suspicion everywhere we go. The name of this country has become synonymous with dishonesty. I cannot ....."

Our conversation was brutally interrupted by a knock on the door. I glanced at the clock on the wall and it read 22:20. My friend and I threw surprised glances at each other.

"Who could be knocking on my door at this hour of the night?" Paul asked.

"If you don't go by the door and enquire, you'll never know," I responded.

He moved to the door and asked who it was.

"It's me Fred, the friend of Johnson," a voice answered from outside.

The name Johnson assured Paul that the visitor outside was not going to be an unusual one. Johnson was the name of his elder brother. Anxious to welcome his elder brother's friend and to find out what news or item his brother must have sent for him, he opened the door. He was grossly mistaken. The mouth of a pistol was put on his forehead. He started reversing with his hands up. There were three young men dressed in jeans and masks. Paul reversed right to the centre of the sitting room where they asked him to lie down. He obeyed quickly. I lay on the couch on my back watching

TV but as they made their way in, I backed the ceiling and buried my face in my hands.

"Good boy," one of them said as he saw me with my face down.

"Carry the radio set with the TV and deck," the one with the gun ordered.

The two others obeyed. They carried the radio set out first and then came back for the TV and the deck. One of them who went for the TV drew the attention of the others to the name written on the screen by gesturing.

"Who among you two is the owner of this house?" the one with the gun asked.

"I'm the one," Paul indicated.

The one with the gun ordered Paul to get up and he pulled him by the ear to where the TV was.

"What is the meaning of this?" the thief asked Paul.

"I don't understand sir… the meaning of what?" he asked.

"Who asked you to write your name on this screen," the thief asked again giving him a hard kick.

"Sorry sir, I will never do it again," he promised.

"Next time, when you want to buy valuable things, remember that people like us are out there and need our share. So, don't write your name again on them. Do you understand?" the thief asked.

"Yes sir," Paul answered.

The thief with the gun was the only one left in the house as the other two were probably waiting for him outside. He threatened to shoot us if we tried to raise an alarm and asked us to count from one to thirty. While we were counting, he moved out of the sitting room through the main door. Immediately he was out of the house, a car drove off very fast. There was no need to raise an alarm. Even if we did call the police, they would have taken hours to come. So, what difference did it make? If there was any iota of sleep in our eyes before the thieves came, I think they stole that too. We found it hard to sleep after their speedy departure. With the TV spared because of the name on it, we continued watching movies till the morning hours of the next day without uttering a word to each other. We did not also bother to wake those who were already asleep. We wanted them to discover everything for themselves in the morning. But we were able to laugh at funny scenes that came up in the different movies. At least, the laughter helped to take away some of the trauma the armed robbers subjected us to. What a hilarious welcome after days out of the city!

At 03:00 the next morning Paul's wife walked into the sitting room from the bedroom. I think she came to find out why her husband decided to spend the night in the there.

"Aaah! What is happening with you two here? Don't you feel as to sleep? What could be happening on TV that would keep you awake all night?" she asked.

None of us offered a word but just stared at her for a few seconds if to say 'if only you knew what had just taken place here,' and continued watching the television. I think she started asking herself questions after our strange behaviour. Then her eyes fell on the spot where the radio set was and she could not find it. The deck too was not in its place.

"Where are the other things there?" she asked pointing to the spots the missing items had occupied some hours earlier before she went to bed.

"A certain 'Sir' came here shortly after you went to bed and took them away," I said.

My response triggered some laughter from Paul but confused his wife even more. It was evident from her looks.

"What is he talking about?" she asked her husband.

"My dear, we had some unusual visitors here last night," Paul told his wife.

"You mean armed robbers?" she asked.

"Exactly my dear" Paul confirmed.

She exclaimed and carried her hands on her head. It was as though her feet could no longer carry her. She sat down for a minute and got up again and moved back to their bedroom. She soon re-emerged and I could hear the sound of doors opening and closing. Then she moved to the sitting room again and went to the door and examined it. There was no evidence of any use of force on it.

"But they didn't break the door," she remarked. How did they get in here?

"Well, Paul actually opened the door for them after they made him believe that they had an important message from a relative and called that relative by name. With such convincing evidence, he just opened the door and was greeted with guns," I explained and went on to enact the whole scene as it took place. I made sure I did not leave out any details. That threw them into laughter especially when I got to the point where one of the thieves went to get the TV set only to discover that Paul had written his name on the screen. Paul's wife laughed to the extent that she had to stretch her body on the couch she was sitting on with tears running down her cheeks. She started pleading with me to stop because her ribs were already hurting. I obeyed because I was worried about her advanced state of pregnancy.

It was already dawn and Paul asked me to follow him outside as he had something important to tell me. He did not have a pleasant look on his face. But how could he after some of his valuable assets had been forcefully taken away from him by some agents of the dark world? I knew what was going through his head at that very moment. I knew he needed someone to air out his feelings to. I followed him out as he had requested.

"Smith, I don't know what is happening to me. I don't know if what is happening to me is a result of ill luck or if I've been bewitched or if the devil has put a spell on me. Did my parents or grandparents or great grandparents commit a crime that I do not know of and I'm now paying for? Is someone in the village visiting the witch doctors on my behalf?" he wondered aloud.

"Paul, I've known you for a very long time. Where are you driving to with that line of thought? Do you mean to tell me that you think there is an evil force at work?" I asked.

"Out of the house, I encounter guys with guns and even inside my own house, they still come and meet me. How can you explain that? The worse thing is that they follow me mostly to where I invite you to accompany me. I now have the feeling I'm always putting you in harm's way," he said.

"Paul I understand. But you don't have to feel that way. We are friends and should remain so in good and bad times," I told him.

"Thank you for understanding. You are really a true friend," he said.

"You are welcome. I will always be available anytime you need my help," I reassured him and we moved back into the house. I then informed his wife and the rest of the house that I had to go and see after my own house. They were all very happy that I spent the night with them but sad because of the robbery incident.

I stepped out of Paul's house at exactly 07:05. I started moving down the busy street but I did not pay much attention to what was happening in the street. The phrase 'putting you in harm's way' which was made by my friend only a few minutes earlier preoccupied my mind. I started asking myself so many questions. What did he mean by always putting me in harm's way? Was he trying to put some distance between us? Was he afraid of being accused if something bad happened to me while in his company? I just could not figure out what prompted him to make such a statement. Besides, I've never known him to be superstitious. Superstitious! The word resounded again in my head. The English might have invented the word but they definitely did not acquire the monopoly of giving it meaning. People used it in Cameroon and most of Africa to explain unexpected happenings or things that could not be explained scientifically. Closely related cousins such as sorcery and witchcraft easily fitted in the same shoe. But I thought the advent of modern technology would have eroded some of the superstitious thinking that came from people especially from those who lived in towns like my friend. I was still ruminating over the issue when I heard someone greet me. It was Hansel, Helen's kid brother. He was sixteen and wore a complete sport outfit. I think he was doing his usual morning jogging. His face was not bright and I could sense that something was not in place.

"How are you doing?" I asked hoping he would go straight to what was bothering him.

"All is well," he said looking on the ground.

"All is not well. I can read it all over you. What is wrong? I asked.

He looked at me, took in a deep breath and said "My cell phone has just been stolen."

"When did that happen?" I asked.

"Just this morning as I got into a crowded taxi to head to the play ground where I always go for sports. I got there only to realize that the phone was no longer with me. I did not have the energy to do the sport. So, I've decided to walk home," he said.

"Where did you keep it?" I asked.

"I had it tied to this rope hung round my neck," he said showing me the rope which had been carefully cut by the thief.

"Was the phone the only thing stolen? I asked.

"Yes," he replied.

"Then I don't think it is as bad as you are making it sound. You should be happy that the thieves only stole your phone and left your head with you. Have you thought of what would have happened if they decided to brutalize you before taking it away? By not stealing your head along with the phone, I think those thieves were very generous. They have taken the phone but not your hands, have they?" I asked.

"No," he replied.

"Then, work and buy another one. By hurting over the loss of your phone, you are giving those idiots a reason to celebrate, don't you think? By the way, how is Helen?"

"She is doing fine," he said. "I'm hurrying home to change and go out to check on a friend.

"Okay, I will see you later," I said and continued on my way.

12

I got to my gate at 08:00. I was feeling worried that Helen might have been in the house waiting for me after I called and informed her that I was back the previous day. I began to ask myself what excuse I was going to give her if she tried to find out why I spent the night out. Telling her that I spent the night at Paul's house at his request was going to open an avenue for her to mock me. She would have asked me why I did not just pack and move into Paul's house. My heart pounded as I moved up the steps that led to my house.

I got to the door and touched it after a lot of hesitation. It was locked. I knocked and there was dead silence. I think God was on my side that morning. I unlocked it and went straight to the bathroom. I got out feeling free and light. It was as though I'd washed down a heavy burden which was weighing me down. I moved to my bedroom and fell in bed after locking the door. The ordeal of the previous night came back vividly to my mind. But it was not enough to prevent me from sleeping. I badly needed it and the fatigue resulting from the sleeplessness of the previous night became more of a catalyst.

I had hardly closed my eyes for two hours when I was again brutally awoken by the loud ring tone of my phone. 'Who can it be? I wondered aloud. On picking the phone I could read 'Paul calling' on the screen. It stopped ringing as I delayed in taking the call and I threw it back on the bedside cupboard where it was. I thought that was the end of it but it started ringing again. It was Paul again.

'What could he want at this moment knowing full well that we had not covered our eyes all night and I badly need rest?" I asked myself. There was only one way to find out and so I took his call. When I answered the call, Paul informed me that he had just received a call from his younger brother that his father was critically ill and was lying at the Bamenda General hospital. I could hear the emotion in his voice as he spoke. At that point I felt a bit sorry for him because everything that was happening to him must have certainly been taking a serious toll on his nerves. He was my friend and I agreed to meet up with him in the hospital as fast as I could despite being tired. I got out of bed, got dressed and left the house again.

I got out of the gate and onto the main road and stood there waiting for a taxi. The sun was shining brightly but given that it was in the heart of the rainy season, I could not trust the weather. It was a normal thing for bright sunshine to give way to rain in a matter of minutes. I thought of hiring a commercial motor bike to take me there given that the hospital was just some four kilometres from my house in the eastern part of town. But to get there, one had to go through central town with all the heavy traffic congestion involved. A commercial motor bike could go much faster given that the bike rider could easily meander through small openings between cars. But most of them were inexperienced, had very little knowledge of the highway code and were very reckless on the high way. It was as if they enjoyed riding at high speed and riding slowly was considered a crime. Making the greatest amount of money in the shortest possible time was their top most priority. Their safety and the safety of those they transported didn't seem to matter much. A few years back when the bikes started pouring into the country, the government insisted on the use of safety helmets. A few adverts were made on National Television on the advantages

126

of wearing a helmet. Law enforcement officers were sometimes sent out to ensure that bike riders respected the law. Unfortunately, when defaulters were caught, money simply changed hands and everything went back to normal. Due to the mess involved, the brilliant campaign simply died a natural death and nobody cared about it anymore. Accidents involving bike riders became too frequent. Recklessness had become the norm. Most of them over took on the right instead of the left as well as in places they should not have such as road bends. The fact that most of them could not make any sense of the white breaking and continuous marks on the road further compounded the situation. Those they transported were the greatest victims most of the time. Only a week earlier, a bike rider and his passenger were crushed under a truck before my very eyes as they were trying to overtake it. Unfortunately for them the car I was in just appeared from the opposite direction and in a bid to escape ended up under the truck. They all died on the spot. We now have an average of six accidents involving bike riders a day in Bamenda town alone. They have made driving in the city difficult, adding to the already numerous existing problems. With those thoughts going through my mind, coupled with the weather factor, I decided not to take a bike. So, a taxi halted in front of me and I got in after making my destination known to the driver.

We started off at 10:25 and just as I had suspected earlier, we got caught up in traffic at central town. Most of the congestion was caused by the traffic police who instead of controlling the traffic, were checking the car documents of taxi drivers and letting private cars go. Those whose car documents were incomplete put a 500 Frs. note or coin among the documents before handing them to the police officer to check. When the police officer opened the documents and saw the note, he simply took it and handed the documents back to the driver without checking them. When the drivers played the game, traffic was smooth but when some got stubborn, things got bad and one could get stuck for hours.

We had been in the same spot for about 20 minutes and soon were on the move again. We moved about 200 meters and stopped again. There were only four taxis in front of us. I could see through the wind screen a policeman talking and pointing his finger in the face of the driver who was in front of him still behind his steering wheel. The driver parked in the middle of the road and it seemed he did not have his tongue in his pocket as he too was shouting back at police officer. I knew there was something wrong with his documents and he did not want to behave. I got curious and wanted to know every detail of what was going on. So, I got out of the taxi and went closer to the scene of action.

"Young man, why are you so stubborn? Can't you see that your insurance expired more than a week ago? You are transporting people and do you know what will happen if you have an accident now and they are wounded? Will you be able to foot the hospital bills alone?" asked the police man.

"I know that my insurance has expired but I have made up my mind not to waste my money paying for car insurance. I have decided to become the insurance. Can you name anybody who has had an accident and has been compensated by the insurance company under which he/she is registered?" the taxi driver asked?

The police officer did not say anything. He just stood there staring at the driver with a very angry look. The driver in question left his steering wheel and moved to the front of his taxi. He then beckoned the police officer who followed him. I also moved to the front to see what he wanted to show the policeman. He showed him new head lights and his bonnet which from every indication had just undergone some repair works.

"Look here, I spent over 200, 000frs to have this repaired. Only last week, a fellow taxi driver was trying to dodge a careless motor bike rider and crossed the road and bump into me on the opposite side of the road. I called my insurance company and do you know what they did? They came and were looking for reasons to make me feel it was my fault so that they would not have to pay me. They succeeded in what they wanted to do and I had to repair my car without the company's help. They are all a bunch of thieves as are those who govern us," he said and moved back to his steering wheel.

At that point the policeman softened his looks and handed back the car documents to him. I think he felt some sympathy for the driver. However, I rushed back to the taxi I was in and we started moving again. The driver did not bother to hold out his car documents. He simply took out a 500 Frs. bank note and held it in his left hand. With the taxi still on the move, he extended his arm and handed the bank note to the policeman and we sped off. It was obvious that other drivers and some pedestrians saw the policeman taking the money but it meant nothing to him since it was already an open national game. I had my eyes fixed on the taxi driver I sat next to without blinking. I think it made him uneasy and he decided to react.

"Please, stop staring at me like that. It was just to save time," he said.

"You are the ones promoting all this bribery and corruption in this country," I told him.

"What do you want me to do? We have wasted already more than 30 minutes there and do you know how much I would have made within that time? This job is the only one I've been able to find after my university studies. Our government happens to be that one which does not create avenues for job openings. It waits for people to suffer and come up with something for themselves and then it would come in claiming to put some order by imposing documents which people must acquire before they continue operating. Look at the commercial motor bike sector for example. Most of those boys involved in that sector are university graduates. Many of them have been out for years with no work. They have decided to get bikes only to survive. The government has come in and has imposed a certain number of documents each of them must possess. Has it ensured that the bike riders go through appropriate training before they start using the roads? That is not important to them. All our government is interested in is the money that will get into the state coffers after the bike riders pay for the documents that have been imposed on them. What happens to the money at the end? It is either embezzled or stolen or put in private bank accounts outside this country. That should tell you that we have a government that is out to exploit and reap where it didn't sow. They pretended to impose the wearing of helmets claiming that they wanted to ensure the security of the citizens. How many motor bikes have been impounded because the riders do not have helmets? They are not serious about it because they have nothing to benefit from it. Policemen are taking advantage of it to make money for themselves. That is our country which allows those in positions of power to prey on the poor struggling citizens. Can you really blame me for doing what I did?" he asked.

I did not respond and asked him to drop the topic. It was too nerve breaking for me particularly as I knew the harm corruption was doing to my community and my country and those who suffered the long term consequences. Sleep was quickly taking hold of me and I hadn't the energy to fight it. I soon dosed off.

I could feel someone's arm on my shoulder shaking and asking me to wake up. I opened my eyes and realized it was the taxi driver and we were already in front of the hospital gate. I paid, thanked him and rushed to the reception hall where I hoped to find Paul. There were so many patients waiting to be attended to. The patients had to pay their consultation fees there at the reception before they were told where to go to be consulted. Anyone who did not have the fee was left there and nobody cared to ask what he/she wanted or was doing there. There were three rows of benches which were all occupied. I glanced through the hall and Paul was nowhere to be found. I saw an elderly man sitting in the first row. I think he must have been in his late 60s. His face was buried in his palms with his elbows resting on his lap. He had a dejected look on his face. Anybody entering the reception could see that. A young girl, about 14 years old sat next to him. I think she was his daughter. I looked at her legs and could see black scars on them. Her fair skin colour made the scars even more visible. Within the scars were projected edges of cable wires. That was not normal and I went closer to take a look. I saw that the projected edges of wires were accompanied by some whitish substances which even a half blind person could see. At first glance, one would have thought that the young girl was suffering from chicken pox. I imagined that the girl had been tortured but was not certain yet. There was no need to let my curiosity have the better of me at that moment given that she was not the reason for my presence in the hospital. I felt that it was better to spot Paul first. So, I got out of the reception and rang Paul on his mobile phone. He told me he was in the private ward next to the female accident ward. I knew where that was and headed straight there. I found him outside the ward waiting for me.

"Thank you for coming my friend. In fact, it never rains but it pours. Who would have believed that after the long journey and last night's incident, we would be here again this morning?" he asked.

"Nothing will come to you that you cannot shoulder," I said. "By the way, how is he doing and what is he suffering from?" I asked.

"We don't know yet. Tests are still being conducted. So, we are still waiting," he said.

I got into the room in which Paul's father was and saw him lying on one of the four beds found in the room, though it was called a private ward. He was asleep and I did not want to bother him. I sat near his bed for a few minutes observing him. He was breathing heavily and the three other patients in the room and their relatives were feeling uncomfortable with it, though they did not want us to notice it. I soon realized that the test results from the lab might take some time to come and decided to go back to the reception hall to learn what happened to the young girl I saw with wire edges in her skin.

When I got there I saw the old man and his daughter still sitting on the same spot I left them with a good number of those who came after them no longer there. I walked up to the receptionist to find out why the old man and his daughter had not been attended to.

"They don't have money for the doctor's pen," the lady there told me without bothering to look at me.

Like a man in a confused state of mind, I repeated the young lady's words almost unconsciously. "Is that what you call consultation fee now?" I asked.

"No, the consultation fee is apart and money for the doctor's pen is an extra 300 Frs. the patients have to add to it," she explained.

"Do you issue receipts for the amount paid for the doctor's pen?" I asked.

She did not respond immediately. She looked at me for a few seconds and went back to what she was doing. I think I was already irritating her with my questions.

"Madame, I've asked you a question. Do you issue receipts for the extra money patients pay?" I asked again

"No!" she replied.

"So tell me, are you here to save lives first or to make money?" I asked.

"I am just following instructions," she said

I went to the girl who sat next to the old man and took the exercise book she held in her hand with the 1500 Frs. official consultation fee and slammed it on the receptionist's desk. "If you don't take care of this immediately, something else will happen here today," I warned and went back to meet the old man.

After about four minutes, she beckoned the young girl and handed the exercise book to her alongside a consultation fee receipt. She then asked the girl to go to room 14. I sat next to the old man to get answers to the numerous questions that were running through my mind.

"Is that your daughter?" I asked.

"Yes my son," he replied.

"What happened to her?" I asked

"My son, the world is wicked. Indeed, it is wicked," he began. "I am now an old man and can no longer provide for my large family. I have three wives and eighteen children. That one you saw here is just one of them. She is barely 15. A year ago, a couple that happened to be natives of my village but live in the capital City came around looking for a housemaid. I saw it as an opportunity to raise some money with which I could use to buy some food and feed my family. They made a very generous offer which I found hard to turn down," he explained.

"What did they promise you?" I asked.

He sat still for a moment, turned and looked at me and opened his mouth but the words got stuck in his throat. Tears began streaming down his eyes. He pulled himself together and continued.

"They promised they were going to send us 10.000 Frs. every month as well as send my daughter to school. I could not turn down such an offer because I did not have the means to send my children to school. Besides, since the couple was from my village, I believed in them and thought that they would treat my daughter as their own sister. But I was wrong," he said wiping off a tear that was making its way down his right cheek.

"What did your daughter tell you when she got back?" I asked.

"You just saw her. You saw the scars and the small cable wires in her flesh and the puss coming out. She told me that it was the man's wife who did all that to her. She said each time the man came home for lunch break and there was nobody at home, he would drag her into his bedroom and rape her. She told me it was last month that the man's wife unexpectedly came home and caught her and the man in bed. Instead of confronting her husband, she decided to take out her anger on my daughter. The man's wife accused her of seducing as well as trying to take her husband. My daughter said she used electric cable wire to beat her. I think that explains why she has some of the pieces in her flesh," he explained.

"So, is it the couple that decided to send her back?" I asked.

"My daughter told me that after the beatings, she was not allowed to venture out of the gate. She became a prisoner and was no longer given food and fed only on leftovers. If she's here today, it's because she escaped. She told me she had to wash her master's clothes and saw 10.000 Frs. in one of his trousers. It is the money she used to find her way back here. We even used part of it to pay the consultation fee," he said.

"Have they called or come to find out if she is here with you?" I asked.

"Not at all," he replied. "Loretta told me she does not think they would bother to look for her.

"Who is Loretta?" I asked.

"She is the one who has gone for consultation," he told me.

"Was she communicating with you while she was there?" I enquired.

"I often called her on the woman's mobile phone and she always told me that all was well," he said.

"But what did you expect? Did you expect her to tell you that she was being maltreated when the woman was probably nearby listening?" I asked.

"My son, what do you want me to tell you? The changing time has imposed a lot of hardship on me. I love all my children but I now see it was better to have just a few of them whom I could feed and send to school," he said almost crying again.

"Did you go to the police to report what had happened to your daughter?" I asked.

The old man turned and stared me straight in the eyes for a few seconds then started looking at the floor and tapping his right leg.

"Did you say the police?" he asked looking really curious. "You give me the impression that you don't live in this country. Look at me, really take a closer look at me, I am just a poor man with nothing. Those fellows who maltreated my daughter have all the money in the world to bribe the police and even the courts. What would you want me to go and do there? I have nothing to do there. Justice is not for the poor," he said shaking his head in frustration.

Just then, Loretta walked in holding her consultation book. I looked at the scars and saw that the pieces of wire had been extracted. I also took the consultation book and saw that she was prescribed four different types of drugs. I asked them to wait for me at that reception room. I rushed to the hospital pharmacy, bought the drugs which were not expensive and returned.

"My son, you are really God sent. God will bless you abundantly. The world needs more people like you," he said going down on his knees.

"Please, don't do that," I protested. "It was just a normal thing to do.

"What can I do to thank you or show my gratitude to you?" he asked.

"You can thank me by taking good care of your daughter and children as a whole and not allowing anyone to maltreat them. If they are to starve, you should starve with them. By the way, there is another patient over there I would like to check on," I said and started moving away.

"God bless you my son," he shouted after me.

I got to the private ward and met Paul sitting outside on a bench so dejected with red eyes.

"What is wrong? Were you told that your father has a few days to live?" I asked.

Paul did not offer a word but instead handed the lab test results to me. Everything was negative. I found it hard to believe.

"How can they say everything is negative when that man is lying there helpless? Are they sure they carried out the right tests?" I wondered aloud.

"That is what is beating my imagination and I've just been asking the same question," Paul said. "I can't believe that they are unable to discover what is wrong with my father. How could they discover when they bribed their way into the Higher Institute of Medicine and bribed their way through examinations? Today they are putting on white robes and passing around as doctors....doctors my foot. Killers...that is what they are, trained killers. I don't know why my brothers brought him here. They should have taken him to one of those mission hospitals even though they are expensive. There at least, you spend the money with the conviction that you will eventually get better. But here, what a mess! You are never sure of anything. They are only interested in making money. They now use the lab as a means of making money. Only last week, Mr. Kimmer's daughter who studies at St Jude High School came to me and complained of fever and I sent her here only for her to return and tell me that she was sent to the lab. The money she had to use to purchase drugs went for lab results which were negative of course. But she was prescribed drugs all the same... for malaria. I don't blame them, I blame the system which promotes lawlessness. The medical practitioners are free to do whatever they want without accountability. Patients come here and die out of sheer negligence and nobody is held accountable. Hospitals have now been transformed into business enterprises. Mmm... you need to see them on their graduation day, all dressed up in immaculate white robes, going to take hypocritical vows. You would think they are real human beings whereas they are messengers of the devil. I think they are now trying to recover all the money they used in bribing their way into the core and the patients are the ones paying with their lives. What a..."

I had decided to let him air out his frustration without interruption but soon glanced at my watch and stopped him before he completed his last sentence.

"I agree with all that you are saying but I don't think your criticisms are going to cure that man lying on that bed. Take him to a mission hospital and after that you will have all the time to make all the criticisms you want," I said.

"I'm sorry. I allowed myself to be carried away by my frustration. Could you please help me to hire a taxi so that we can take him to St Mary Health centre?" he requested.

"Sure, I'll do just that," I replied and dashed out of the hospital.

Finding a taxi was not a problem especially when I used the word 'hire'. Some drivers would have preferred to drop all their passengers when such a situation presented itself. I knew the inconveniences involved in boarding a taxi and then

138

being abandoned midway. So, I went for one that I saw was completely empty. Paul's father was brought out on a stretcher and put in the front seat next to the driver. We bent the seat backward such that it looked almost like a bed. In 10 minutes, we were at St Mary. The driver hooted on his way into the hospital premises to indicate that he was bringing in a patient whose situation was critical. Before we grinned to a halt, there were already three nurses waiting with a stretcher. He was taken into a private ward and laid on the only bed we saw in the room. A doctor immediately walked in and began examining him. Paul handed the lab results of the series of tests conducted at the provincial hospital on him. Paul also informed the doctor that his father could not talk or even turn on the bed by himself. The doctor, on carrying out his examination, discovered that Paul's father could not turn his neck either left or right. The doctor then sent for a lab technician who came and got his blood sample and went to carry out some tests. The doctor then requested for a new exercise book in which he could pen down his diagnosis and prescriptions. Paul's younger brother, Charles was sent for the book.

A few minutes later, Charles came in with the exercise book and handed it to the doctor.

"What name should I write on it?" he asked.

"Mr. Fru Jones," Paul replied.

The doctor left the room and we sat there anxiously waiting for what would come out of the lab. Close to one and a half hours later, we saw the doctor returning with the lab results from a distance.

"I have the feeling things are not going to be good," Paul whispered to me.

"Let's just wait and hear what news he has for us," I told him as we watched the doctor come closer. When he got to the door, Paul's elder brother, Fredrick, was the first to face him.

"What is wrong with my father?" he asked as we all closed in on the doctor to hear what he had to say.

"Gentlemen, you all have to be brave," he said. "I'm sorry I don't have good news for you. Your father has been diagnosed with meningitis. It is already at a very advanced stage. I'm afraid you brought him here too late. His spinal cord has been badly affected. There's not much we can do for him right now. I'm sorry," he added and turned to leave.

"Please doctor, is there absolutely nothing you can do for my father?" he asked almost in tears.

"We will do all we can for him but I'm not promising you anything. But I think we will need a miracle at this point. Please pray for your father and pray hard. He will need your prayers," he said as he moved away.

Paul and I felt disconsolate after the doctor left. We all understood that Paul's father had come to the end of the road except Fredrick who was a staunch traditionalist who believed in traditional herbal medicine. As far as formal education was concerned, he did not go far and I doubted if he made anything out of what the doctor said. But he at least understood what the doctor meant by 'not being able to do much for his father'.

"If these people cannot do anything for father, we should take him to Pa Ngom at Nsam hillside so that he can prepare some good herbal concoction for him. I don't know why he had to be brought here in the first place," Fredrick said.

"At this point I don't think that any idea should be shoved aside. We all want the same thing and it is that father

140

should get back on his feet. In that case then, I will give you some money so that you take him and go ahead while I get back to my house and put some things in place and meet up with you tomorrow," Paul said handing him 40,000 Frs.

"Thank you for all that you are doing for our family. You go and take care of your things. I will handle everything from here," he said.

Paul and I went to the doctor and told him of the plan B which had been adopted. The doctor asked us to leave him there for a day or two for him to see what he could do before we moved on with the second plan. We had no problem with that and went back to Fredrick to let him know. We decided to go home after that.

13

Once out of the hospital premises, we boarded a taxi and occupied the back seat. It was bound for central town and there were already two other passengers in the cab, one in front next to the driver and the other at the back. In all, we were three passengers that occupied the back seat. The passenger next to the passenger happened to be George, one of our school mates. He found work with a road construction company. He had his company clothes on.

"Hi George, long time no see. I see you in your company attire. Are you going to do some company work or are you returning from an errand?" Paul asked.

"I'm coming from the hospital," he replied.

"Are you sick or you did go to check on a patient?" I asked.

"I went there to see my twin brother," he said.

"What is he suffering from…chronic constipation? Paul asked jokingly.

"No," he replied laughing. "He had a malaise yesterday.

"A malaise!!!" Paul and I exclaimed at the same time.

"What happened?" I asked.

"You see, my brother is a young man who believes so much in himself and would not listen to me his elder simply because we have less than minutes age difference. He is a handsome young man, even more handsome than I am and is aware of it. With that idea in his head, he does not believe that there is any woman in this country who can turn him down. He is after all 'God's gift to women," he said with a cynical look on his face.

"Wait, is that what he calls himself?" I asked.

"Don't mind him," George replied. "So, he met this girl, Laura, four months ago. She is a girl of average physical beauty and is very aware of that fact. If all women were like her, I'm sure they wouldn't be falling prey to dubious men. But my brother, a chronic womanizer, saw her and started telling her how she was the most beautiful and attractive girl on the face of the earth. To make himself even more ridiculous, he told her that he loves her to the extent that he is prepared to go to hell with her rather than to heaven alone. True, those are the type of things women love to hear but not all. He had no intention of going even a mile with her and he betrayed himself by asking her to bed less than a week after they met. Being an intelligent girl, she read his moves very fast and would not give in. All the while, he has been showering her with gifts... money... taking her to night clubs... all in a bid to get her into his bed. He even tried to get her drunk so that he could get what he wanted. But, she has always been on her guard. She came and explained things to me and I understood that she is a woman of dignity and would do everything possible to stay that way. I tried to talk some sense into my brother, but he wouldn't listen. Instead he accused me of being too local in my deeds and way of reasoning. What happened yesterday was the straw that broke the camel's back. He tried to use force to sleep with her and Laura got angry and told him that he wasn't man enough for her. That is what made my brother almost have a heart attack. He could not believe that he had been given a cold shoulder by a girl who in his own words "was not even beautiful." For the first time in his life, my bother preferred death."

We all exploded with laughter including the cab driver.

"So, he wanted to die simply because a woman turned him down?" Paul asked.

"What answer do you want me to give you? The disgrace must simply have been too much for him to bear," George said laughing.

"How is he doing now?" I asked.

"He is doing much better now. I think he will get out in three days. The doctors said that they want to keep him again under observation," he said with emotion mounting in his voice. "When I asked him to stop womanizing, he would call me a local man. See where it has landed him... with all the deadly diseases that are transmitted sexually especially HIV/AIDS. What kind of brother do I have that does not want to take to advice? Now he is just lying on that hospital bed comfortably and only giving orders... buy me this and buy me that... I'm the one footing the bills. I am just waiting for him to get well first. When he gets out of that hospital, I will teach him a lesson."

We were fast approaching central town with its dense traffic congestion. The taxi soon came to a halt and George had to alight as he was already outside the company premises.

"I will see you guys some other time" he said and left.

When he got out, the passenger who sat directly behind the driver started laughing.

What is funny?" Paul asked.

"I'm still thinking of the story that that brother who just went out narrated a while ago. Is that his brother living with him?" he asked.

"Yes," I replied.

"Who pays for the house?" he asked.

"Nobody pays for the house. In fact, that one who went out owns the house," I replied.

"Does his twin brother work?" he asked.

"Why all these questions, are you a cop or something?" Paul asked.

"Please, just answer the question. You don't know what I'm driving at," he said.

"Yes," I replied without stating the type of work.

"I'm sorry but I think your friend is not helping his twin brother grow. I don't see why he should still be housing a full grown man who is working like that. If a man is able to date a woman, he should be capable of doing things independently. If he wants his brother to be responsible, he should ask him to go and rent and why not get a wife. What else do you think he needs to be responsible?" he asked.

What he said made a lot of sense but asking George to send his twin brother out to go and live on his own was another problem. Paul and I as well as many other people had talked to him about keeping his brother and his response had always been that he needed to keep an eye on him. Since we were just friends and total strangers, there was nothing we could do.

It was 13:50 when we got to central town. We decided to alight there and continue on foot though our various homes were still far off. About 600 meters from where we alighted, we met a young man probably in his mid-twenties carrying some twins. They were crying seriously, probably from hunger. The young man, overtaken by events, started crying too. Some idle bystanders and some passers-by laughed at him while others sympathized with him. In the days of old, only the cry of a baby was enough to make any woman abandon whatever she was doing to see what was wrong. But in these modern times with the pace of life going at the speed of light, poverty and hardship had made life a battle for

146

survival thereby eroding the old tradition. Collective solidarity had given way to individualistic tendencies with everyone minding only his or her own business. That explained why some comments were directed at him as he moved along with his babies.

"If you know that you are poor, get a rope and tie that thing between your legs. Or better still don't engage in unprotected sex," a voice said.

Paul and I by passed him and went for about some 200 meters because we were in a hurry to go and get some sleep. A voice within me would not let me be. It kept telling me to go back and see what I could do to assist the young man. I tried to ignore the inner voice but the more I tried to increase the distance between me and the distressed young man, the more guilt built up inside me. I could not understand why. After a few more steps, I decided to stop. Paul was taken aback.

"Why are you stopping?" he asked.

"I don't think we should have left that young man in the state we met him," I said.

"We've by-passed him already. Don't tell me you want to go back there because I'm not coming with you. I'm very tired and need to sleep," he said.

"I am not asking you to come with me. You go ahead and I will call you early tomorrow morning," I said making a u-turn.

I had hardly gone 150 meters when I heard "Wait for me... wait for me..." I turned round and saw that it was Paul. I halted and he caught up with me after a few seconds.

"I thought..."

He did not allow me complete my sentence. He already knew what I was going to say.

147

"Reserve those questions for some other time. Let's just go," he said.

We caught up with the young man at the City Chemist Roundabout. One of the babies had fallen asleep while the other was still crying. The young man too had stopped crying but the paths of his tears were still very much visible on his face. The first thing to do was to relieve him of the babies as we had the feeling that his arms must have been hurting terribly. We did just that.

"Where are you going?" I asked.

"I'm going to G.R.A to my elder sister who is a government worker to see if she can assist me," he said and started crying again.

"Come on, be a man and stop crying. That will not solve your problem. What is your name?" Paul asked.

"Chi Juan," he replied.

"Are these your kids?" I asked.

"Yes," he replied.

"They are lovely," Paul said.

"How old are they?" I asked.

"Five months and three weeks," he replied.

"Where is their mother?" Paul asked.

" As of now, I don't know her whereabouts. I went to work three days ago early in the morning. While I was at my jobsite, I received a phone call from their mother. She informed me that one of the children was very sick. I pleaded with my boss who gave me permission to go home that morning. When I got there, I met only the children and she was nowhere to be found," he explained.

"So, you've been with them for the past three days and their mother has not turned up. How have you been feeding them?" I asked.

"With artificial milk and they finished it this morning," he said.

We understood at once the predicaments he found himself in. At that juncture the baby girl I was carrying stopped crying. I walked into a nearby provision store and bought a 1.5 litres of mineral water. I gave some to her to drink. She drank hungrily and I felt sorry for her. But then I knew doctors had a different opinion of giving water to children below the age of six months. At that moment there was no alternative. The baby Paul carried also woke up. We gave him the water as well.

"What kind of work do you do?" Paul asked.

"I'm a cleaner and servant in a small restaurant in town. I'm paid 15.000 Frs. at the end of the month which does not even come regularly. Feeding myself alone is sometimes not easy let alone paying for the one room I live in," he said with tears trickling down his eyes.

"Well, you said you wanted to go and see your elder sister, right?" I asked.

He simply said yes by nodding.

"That is good for a start but I wonder how long your sister will be able to support you. I know government workers are not well paid because I happen to be one. She must certainly have a family to take care of with very limited resources and you, with these children, might just be another burden, don't you think?" I asked.

He did not say anything. He just stood there confused, tired, overwhelmed by events and not knowing what to do next.

"Go and see her. Even if she cannot help you, she will at least know what you are going through. After seeing your sister you should go to the social welfare. They are there for situations like yours. I only hope they are there to assist and not deceive the outside world to get what they can fill their stomachs with. Nothing seems to be functioning properly in this country anymore. All the same go and explain things there as they happened and they will (should?) help you...one never knows. You could as well go to a parish priest. Collections are always made once in a while meant for helping the needy," I advised.

Since we were at a roundabout, finding a taxi bound for GRA was not going to be difficult. Paul and I contributed 10.000 Frs. and gave it to the father of the twins. The first taxi driver we stopped agreed to take them to their destination. He entered first in the back seat and Paul gave the male child to him. I bent to give the female child I carried and could hear the driver ask Juan where the mother of the children was. He responded that she was at home. I did not expect him to start narrating his story to any Tom, Dick and Harry and so, could not blame him for lying to the driver. I don't think you would have blamed him either, would you?

"God will bless you," he said as the taxi he drove off.

14

Paul and I started off again on our way back home. We boarded different taxis because we lived in different parts of town. It took me 25 minutes to get home. I entered my gate and saw that my door was open. My heart was beating fast as I had no excuse for leaving the house without informing Helen of where I was going either in a written note or phone call. That was my greatest shortcoming. When something hot was at stake, I just took off without leaving any message or telling anyone.

I climbed the steps and got into the house. Helen had put everything in order and was in the kitchen cooking. When she heard footsteps in the sitting room, she got out of the kitchen and threw her arms around me. I held her tight too but many questions started running through my mind. She never spared me when I did anything wrong even if it was very minute. That she just came out and threw her arms around me without first firing at me verbally was very strange. 'Did she just want to welcome me first and fire at me after that? ... Or had she been having some serious thoughts of late? ... Or had someone been schooling her?' I wondered as I held her in my arms. Only time could give answers to my questions. She returned to the kitchen after finding out how I was doing. She did not have the slightest idea of what my friend was going through and I did not want to tell her anything at that moment. What I needed most was sleep so that I could regain form. I went and turned on the TV but did not have time to watch it as I fell asleep on the couch I laid on.

I woke up at 19:00 and went to the bathroom. I came out a few minutes later and went to the dining table which was already set. Helen was sleeping in the bedroom. I went and woke her up and we moved to the table. While savouring the yam and Ndole she prepared, I recounted the previous night's ordeal and everything I saw and heard in the hospital. We sat and watched TV for a short while and then went to bed.

Early the next morning, I informed Helen that there was a possibility that I was going to travel again given the health situation of my friend's father. She got my cell phone and rang Paul to show her concern. He informed her that he was on his way to the hospital to see if his father's situation had improved. She promised that she was going to stop by later in the afternoon. Since I was going to go with her, there was no need asking for the ward or room description. She immediately went to the kitchen after she made the call to prepare what we would take to the hospital when visiting the patient. It was not proper to visit someone in the hospital empty handed.

At 13:40, we left the house for the hospital. We got outside the ward that Paul's father was in and found Paul outside looking very sad. I already knew the condition following what the doctor said the previous day but seeing my friend looking so sad made me imagine the worse.

"Is there any improvement?" I asked.

My friend took a deep breath before opening his mouth to speak.

"I think the old man has come to the end of the road. His situation has not improved even a little. There is no need to wait here. I've asked my elder brother to go on with his plan though I am very sceptical about it. Even if the old man is going to die, it should not be here but in the village. It will be too costly to transport him if he dies here. My elder brother is out there trying to make arrangements to take him to the village," he said with a sigh.

I knew that was a very trying moment for him and his family and he needed all the moral support he could get. I told him he could always count on me for anything. He thanked me for what I said. However, Helen and I entered the ward to see my friend's father. He just laid on the bed as if he was already dead. He looked very helpless. The sight was just too painful and I went out and joined my friend. It was obvious that the old man was not going to eat the food we brought given his helpless state. I asked my friend if his father had eaten anything and he told me that they made everything he had to eat watery before pushing it down his throat using a tube.. That already was not a good sign. Paul's younger brother ate part of what we brought and the rest was given to the other patients who were in the next room.

Fredrick soon returned and his father was taken out on a stretcher by some four male nurses right outside the hospital gate. There, he was lifted and put in the waiting taxi that Fredrick hired. His kid brother who was there entered in the back to help support their father. Fredrick told Paul that since his wife was in a delicate state, it was better for him to stay back and take care of her first given that he was not the medical doctor or traditional healer who would save their father. He promised to call and inform Paul of the latest developments when they got to the village. With that said, they left. Paul and I went back to our separate homes.

Three days after the departure of Fredrick and his critically ill father to the village, we did not hear anything from him. He promised that he was going to call with the latest development and since he did not, Paul and I began imagining that a miracle could not totally be rolled out. But that was no reason to carry our hopes up too high just then. It was important that we saw his father before developing any hopes. But if my friend decided to call his elder brother to find out about the status of their father, it was possible he was going to get him only by chance. The network coverage in their village was not uniform and anyone who had to make a call from there had to get up some elevated ground. It was only Fredrick who could call Paul and if Paul couldn't get through to his brother to get information about their father, he was obliged to go there. For that reason we could not continue waiting and scheduled to travel on the fourth day after Paul's father was taken to the village which was a Saturday.

That Saturday was to come less than 24 hours from the moment we planned to go on the trip. At 06:50 on the day in question I was in the bathroom having a bath when my phone rang. Helen brought it to me and it was Paul trying to reach me. During our conversation, he informed me that he was going to meet me at my house so that we could leave for Nkwen Park together. I told him that I would be waiting for him.

He soon arrived and we left for Nkwen Park. We arrived there at 06:45 and the first bus was almost full and ready to leave. We boarded it after paying and obtaining our tickets. The Toyota Coaster bus hit the road at exactly 07:00. Unlike the road to William's village, that which led to Paul's village was well tarred. We did not have to transfer because the bus we boarded in town was to be the same one that would take us to our final destination. When the bus started off, there was some music playing. Just after about two kilometres, the majority of the passengers started protesting and asking the driver to turn off the radio. Those who protested either had books or newspapers which they wanted to read. The noise was therefore disturbing them or so I thought. The bus driver turned it off as most of the passengers had requested. The bus became too quiet and the only noise one could hear was that made by the car engine. I soon realized that all those that were either reading novels or newspapers were from Paul's village. They were known all over the country as 'great intellectuals'. So, wherever they went they carried along books or newspapers. They made sure they sat where people could see them when they were reading. This was to keep the name of the village and its pride up. The journey soon became boring and I had no intention of regretting that I chose to accompany my friend. I decided to break the silence.

"How come the road to Bokum village is tarred better than those in the rest of this province? Why is Bokum favoured over the rest? " I asked targeting no one in particular.

My question left nobody indifferent. It was a very sensitive question and touched the very heart of their pride. Everyone stopped reading and all attention was focused on Paul. The self appointed spokesman stood up and moved to the only door that passengers used to get enter and exit the bus. There, he held the locked door to avoid being knocked off his feet. Certain that he was in a position where everyone could see him, he adjusted his attire and posture to look like that of a proud minister who saw himself as a demi-god going to address an illiterate community. That provoked some laughter.

"Do you really want to know why?" he asked.

"Of course, that is the reason why I asked the question in the first place," I said.

"Well, I will tell you," he began...You know we are the most educated people in this country. As testimony to that fact, you will always see people from my village with either books or newspapers. The knowledge we acquiring arms and prepares us to better face the situations that come ahead of us. The kind of government we have is one of the problems we have learnt to deal with. We've realized that the development we badly need cannot come if we stand on the side of the government. We are dealing with a government which is, pardon my expression, calculative but stupid, confused, lacks foresight and has no clear cut development plans for this country. They reason and see things only in terms of elections. All they care about is how to stay in power and they pretend to do things only when an election is around the corner. It has been struggling to get us on its band wagon so that it can easily get hold of some of the minerals our village is sitting on. We, being so wise, have vowed to always be on the side of the opposition so that we can prey on the desperation of this government which reasons only along political lines, to demand whatever we want and it will be given. Look at some of the neighbouring villages that decided to join the ruling party... development is no longer coming because the government is no longer wooing them. They can't boast of what we have such as good roads, schools, a well equipped medical facility though it is understaffed, and constant electricity supply. These are all things that are supposed to be provided for, without us asking for them so long as we pay our taxes. But such is not the case. Those in the neighbouring villages are now regretting why they joined the government. Now the government goes there only to tap out their resources, plus the taxes they pay, without giving them anything in return. When the government wants to appease them after receiving many complaints and threats, it appoints one of theirs to a high post of responsibility and most of them being uneducated, will be contented. The person appointed will use his post as evidence to convince the poorly educated villagers that the government is thinking of them. They sheepishly vote and maintain the same government in office and the same process begins again. Who benefits from appointments? The truth is that only those that are appointed and their families benefit. Do the villagers in their vast majority benefit anything? They benefit very little. That is why education is good and we have decided not to build mansions and buy expensive flashy cars but to send our children to school. Those who are uneducated will always be used like tools and we cannot fall into that category. The worse thing that God can do to someone is to deny him or her brains. But everybody alive have been given one but most people have preferred to turn theirs into pillows on which they sleep and allow an insignificant few to reason for them. We will not allow that to happen to our children and that is why we, the people of Bokum village would prefer to walk around in rags and use the money we make to educate our children. We want every Bokum son and daughter to be able to reason for his or herself and not see things through the eyes of some greedy and selfish politicians. Politicians are never to be trusted. When they want to get elected into office, they make a million promises. Once they are in office, they will start giving a billion excuses on why they are unable to fulfil their promises. They sheepishly stick to the colonial ideology that problems in politics are never solved but moved or postponed. Those same people who brought that ideology, whom we fought and drove away, have come back and our leaders have given them our lands which they are exploiting and using the resources to solve problems back in their home countries while we are here postponing ours. Since our government is not courageous enough to face the former colonial master and has decided to remain its puppet, we wouldn't want it to come and try to outwit us with its empty promises. That is why education is very important and knowledge is power. If the government decides to use force, with our knowledge, we would know how to fight back.

That long explanation attracted a thunderous round of applause from the natives of his village and some of them shouted 'you are a true son of the soil'. I admired the people for their attachment to their village and what they believed in. I imagined that our country would have been a paradise if all the people behaved like them. But that was all wishful thinking because people will always reason differently especially when self interest has an upper hand.

15

We got into the village at 13:00 and alighted after a sign board which indicated that we were within Bokum village territory. Paul suggested that we get on motorbikes to go to their family compound at the eastern side of the village below the foot of a hill. I did not like the idea because I wanted to feed my eyes on the beautiful attractions that the village could offer. I preferred going on foot given the small size of the village. But then, I remembered that we were there to check on his sick father and therefore felt obliged. Without wasting any more time we jumped on two separate bikes and took off towards the village square. It took us ten minutes to get there because the bike riders were speeding as though they were competing with each other. From time to time, I would tap the bike rider who was transporting me on the shoulder and he would slow down. But after a few seconds, he would be back at full speed. I think he was a speed addict.

As we got to the village square, we had to take the road leading to the eastern part of the village. Just about 50 meters from there, we passed an electric pole on which a picture was posted. It looked like that of Paul's father. We did not stop to take a closer look. We continued and came across a second one posted on the wall of a house beside the road. We decided to stop and went to have a closer look. Behold, it was the picture of Paul's father. Paul became weak and was unable to stand on his feet. The bike rider who was transporting him helped him onto a stone which was just there by the road side.

"Come on Paul, I know this is hard but you seem to be behaving as if you didn't know this was going to happen...you and I knew that the old man wasn't going to make it... ooh come on... get up and let's go," I urged.

Paul obeyed like a child without retaliating as usual and in 12 minutes, we were at their family compound. Our entrance provoked a lot of mourning from both the villagers and Paul's family members. The wailing from the women and the sorrowful heart tearing words that some uttered made it difficult for one to hold back his or her tears. I was almost crying but immediately realized and started comforting my friend instead whose shirt was already wet. Among the mourners, there was one who was not happy with what I was doing and walked up to me. He was well advanced in age. I think he must have been in his late 60s.

"Leave that child alone...let him mourn his father. Why are you disturbing him?" he asked.

I did not respond but instead helped my friend into one of the two houses that made up the compound. There I pushed him onto the most comfortable seat so that he could cry out the painful emotions within him. With that done, I went outside to see how the mourners were dramatizing. Just as I stepped out leaving Paul alone, a young woman walked into the compound with a baby strapped to her back. She was shouting at the top of her voice. She threw herself onto the dusty yard still with the baby strapped to her back. Some three fast and hefty men ran to where she fell. While two of them held her, the third man untied the baby and took him away into one of the houses in the compound. She continued rolling on the ground and dirtying herself as the two men let go of her. Some men who sat outside there sipping palm wine were not pleased with the woman's performance and wondered aloud if she wanted to die in the late man's place. They did not understand why she put on such a show as it put the life of the baby she strapped to her back in danger. However, some women rushed and picked her up and the general mourning started again. It lasted for about ten minutes after which, some jugs of palm wine and some crates of beer were brought out. Immediately they were placed at the centre of the yard, all the wailing ceased and all the mourners rushed to get a drink. The whole process started all over each time a new face appeared?. Sometimes when drinks were not brought out after the usual brief moment of shouting and wailing, some of the mourners left the scene disgruntled.

At 15:00, I called one of the mourners by the side of the house where Paul was and asked him where the corpse of the late man was.

"Pa was buried yesterday since there are no fridges here to store dead people as you have in town," he told me.

Paul was definitely not going to be happy with that kind of information but I thought it was important to let him know immediately. So, I went back to the sitting room where I left him and noticed that he had stopped crying and just sat there staring at the picture of his late father on the wall.

"Paulo," I called. "Do you know that your old man was buried yesterday?

"What? Are you sure about this?" he asked. "Why did they not inform me before doing that? Almost all of them here have my phone number. There must be something that is not right here and I have to find out right away."

"Hold on," I stopped him. "It is obvious that you will have a family meeting when the guests have all departed. Why don't you wait and ask all your questions then?"

He thought for a while.

"I think you are right," he said and sat down again.

I sat there by his side and we said nothing to each other but listened to all that was happening outside. We also watched people get into the sitting room and leave. Some who knew Paul came closer to say a few comforting words while others came and threw a glance round the house and left. I did not know why they did that and did not bother to ask. I just felt that there were some actions that one should observe without asking questions.

It was almost 18:00 and people were already retiring to their various homes to prepare for the next day. I was worried about where I was going to spend the night. There were enough rooms but they were going to be occupied mostly by guests who came from afar. Paul had his own room but was forced to give it up for the sake of the guests as well. We both had to find somewhere else to spend the night. We decided to go to a motel that was near the bus stop on the way out of the village. It was 19:00 by my watch.

As we got out of the confines of Paul's family compound, we noticed that bike riders made a little camp just near the gate into the compound. There, they picked up and dropped passengers. Paul and I got on two separate bikes and in 22 minutes, we were at Dreamland Motel. It was not a very large structure. From what I could see, it was built as a living house and then turned into a motel. From where we alighted, there was an open door directly in front of us with the inscription 'Reception' written above it. We walked in and saw that the reception was a large sitting room turned into a bar with a counter full of all sorts of drinks ranging from locally brewed beer to foreign hot whisky. There was a Barman behind the counter who sold drinks, served them and acted as the receptionist at the same time. It was not my place to ask him why he couldn't get someone to assist him, though the urge was there. In front of the counter were tables and chairs and there were some customers too. There was a corridor which led to the various rooms. So, we walked up to the counter and enquired.

"Good evening sir, we are looking for a place to spend the night and are wondering if there are any empty rooms here," Paul said.

"Yes, there are rooms. Do you want to take a single room or two separate rooms?" the receptionist asked.

"Two separate rooms," we both said at once.

"How much will it cost?" I asked.

"6000 Frs.," the receptionist replied.

"Is that for a single room or both?" Paul asked.

"It is for both," he replied.

We both breathed a sigh of relief as he handed to us two separate keys on which the door numbers were attached. I was in a haste to know what the room looked like. I by-passed an army officer who was still in uniform with a young lady sitting on the last table before one stepped into the corridor. They were so intimate. The way they were behaving brought back memories of my first date with Helen. Even after I got into the corridor, I still turned to admire them as I headed to the room. Paul had been observing me and at a certain point shouted at me to take my eyes off the couple. That could, in his words, 'tempt me to do something stupid particularly as I was out of town and far away from Helen'. I got into room 6. Though it was not of my taste, I decided to manage it. At least it was better than spending a night in the open with mosquitoes.

Since it was still too early to go to bed, I decided to go back to the bar and while time by feeding my eyes on the lone TV screen that was found there. I stepped out of my room and saw that Paul had made the same decision too. We went to the bar and again by-passed the romantic couple. Their mood had not changed and we moved to an unoccupied table where we could have a better view. A documentary was going on based on 'why incumbent African heads of state always win in elections'. It was a very interesting documentary but we were not going to follow it up to the end as a woman with a very sharp knife in her right hand made her way into the bar. She wore a complete Addidas sportswear. Physically, she was of average height, fair in complexion and very athletic in structure. She was overtly beautiful. She immediately headed for the table where the romantic couple was having a nice time. Seeing the knife and the rage on the intruder's face, the army officer sprang to his feet and raised his hands upright while the lady with him did same.

"So it is true what people have been telling me… who will wake up my late father from his grave to come and see this?" she exclaimed, crying. "Thomas! Thomas! You have made me a laughing stock in this village… I didn't want to believe any of these things they have been telling me… so it is true…

With the knife in her hand, Paul and I as well as the other customers did not dare try to intervene for fear that she might hurt the lovers. All other activity stopped and all attention was focused on them. Some people came in but no one went out, not because she held them hostage but because they were all trying to figure out how to end the situation without someone getting hurt.

"Thomas! Thomas!" she called out again with tears streaming down her eyes. "Even if you want to cheat on me, you'll not look for someone better? Must you go only for my best friend's second daughter? A girl who does not even have the age of our third child? Thomas, why are you doing this to me?"

Without wasting any more time, the intruder unbuttoned the army officer's trouser with her left hand and brought out his penis which was already erect. Chilling shock waves ran down my spine as I imagined the sharp knife on my own third leg. I got up from where I sat and drew closer cautiously begging her not to do what we imagined she was about to do.

"I will cut this thing so that you'll not be able to disgrace me again," she said without turning to look at me who was pleading from behind. Her comments scared everyone. Paul and I as well as the other customers joined and went further with the begging on our knees. With tears still running down her eyes, she uttered the dreaded words again.

"I will cut it," she said. "The humiliation is too much. How do I face my friend if she finds out about this? I will cut it."

"Please madam, if you do it you'll regret later because he will be of no use even to you," said a voice from behind me. "Please think of your children… just let it go and he will change… think of your children.

It soon became a scenario with us on our knees imploring, and she on her feet threatening. It dragged on for about 20 minutes. At last she surrendered and let go of her husband's penis. He dropped on the floor like a log of wood as soon as he was left alone. The woman left him there with us and walked out of the motel. His lover also left. Some two men lifted the army officer from the floor and placed him back on his seat with his head resting on his folded arms. The other customers hurried back to their various tables and emptied their remaining drinks and left. Paul and I retired to our various rooms though we did not feel like sleeping.

16

The next morning at 07:30, I heard a knock on my door. It was Paul and I asked him to come in.

"Do you want us to leave for your family compound now," I asked.

"Not just yet," he replied. "I just want to tell you that it was hinted by someone yesterday that the general death celebration will take place today. This implies that we, all the children of late Mr. Fru Jones, must each come with a traditional dance group and entertain them after they perform. We, the male children will also have to pay for rounds of gun firing. So, we will have to go at 09:00, first to the compound for me to secure a place where I will entertain my guests and then we will go out to rally some of my friends who will form a dance group or hire one altogether.

"I have no problem with that," I said. "But tell me, why is it someone hinting to you that your father's general death celebration is today? Where are your brothers and sisters? Couldn't they inform you?"

"Brother, just let me be. Honestly, I don't know what is going on. I guess I'm going to find out tomorrow," he said and left my room.

I took advantage of the short time ahead of me to have a bath and settle the bills. I knew we were not going to spend another night in the motel because Paul told me that his father's general death celebration would take place that day. It meant that after all the traditional dance groups had performed, the guests, mourners and sympathizers would depart and there would be enough rooms again in his family compound. The mourning period lasted for just three days. It was in sharp contrast to how long the mourning periods lasted in the past. Mourning periods could last for a whole week if it was just a common man, two or three weeks if it was a title holder, and a month or two if it was a traditional ruler. During the mourning period, guests had to be fed and housed by the family of the deceased. Families that were poor often got insults from the mourners and sometimes were fined by the village council of elders for not respecting the tradition. What a hell that was!

At 09:00 we left the motel for the family compound as we had earlier planned. We got there and realized that a small market was going on just outside the family compound. Young boys and girls of between 10 and 14 years of age as well as women sold items ranging from biscuits to cooked food. Paul looked at them and sighed but did not say or do anything. We just walked on into the compound.

Everyone we met in the compound was busy doing one thing or the other. His brothers and sisters were busy preparing places where they would entertain their guests. Paul did not have a place in their compound. As a result, he went to one of their neighbours (again, be consistent with your writing style. You write mourners in British English but neighbours in American English) and pleaded with him to provide him with a little space where he could entertain his guests only for that day. Mr. Esau, the neighbour and owner of the house agreed. Since the sitting room was already equipped with a set of chairs made of bamboo, we just had to put them in the form of a circle.

At 10:00, the mourners and guests started streaming in. Some of the female mourners brought along food while the men either carried jugs of palm wine or a traditional firearm. All the children of the late man led a traditional dance in the centre of the yard where they would perform for 15-20 minutes and then give way to the next. The first child began and then the second child followed, right down to the last child. During each performance there was intense gun firing. I got curious and asked an old man who was sitting next to me about the significance of such an activity. He looked at me for a short while and then asked me where I came from.

"I'm from Akumo" I told him.

He remained silent for a few minutes and then turned to me again and started explaining why there was intense gun firing.

"It is because people here believe that when someone dies his/her spirit continues to hover around and if there is someone who had problems with the deceased, it is feared that the spirit might take advantage of its invisible nature to get revenge or cause harm. So, that intense gun firing is for the spirit to go far into the spirit world and not hover around in the land of the living", he said.

In the village of people who claimed to be the most educated in the province, his explanation sounded a bit funny to me as I found it really hard to see how people could claim to chase away spirits, which they couldn't see, with guns.

"Thank you for that explanation", I said.

"You are welcome. By the way, why do you ask me why gun shots are fired at funerals? Is it that in Akumo which is just some 74 kilometres away from here such an activity is not carried out?" he asked.

"When I was a kid, I used to see people doing it. But I've never understood why they did it. I just thought that it was part of the funeral ritual or a recipe to make the funeral more interesting. Thanks to you, I now know there is a reason behind it. As I grew older the activity became rarer until it finally died away. It was not so long ago that I got to learn that it was the governor who banned it in the city and the villages outlawed the practice on grounds that it was dangerous to fire guns in densely populated areas.

"Is that the real reason?" he asked. "It was wrong to band such a thing because it is part of our culture. A man without a culture or tradition does not exist. I'm sure he certainly studied out of this continent and was brainwashed while he was out there.

"Pa, I don't think he took (accepted) that decision because he was brainwashed. I just think he was worried about the security of those around and even that of the people firing the guns. Besides, the times are changing and so the traditions have to change too. We cannot see something which is bad and refuse to do away with it because it is tradition. I'm sure you heard of the death of Mr. Soh Stephen," I said.

"Yes, I did," Pa replied. "Death is very cruel, I must say. That man was the most successful businessman this province has ever produced. He was generous, kind and always listened to others.

"Do you know how he died?" I asked

"I heard that his death resulted from an accident though I was never told what kind," he explained.

"Well, I'm going to tell you... It happened at a funeral like this one. That day, he wore this Muslim traditional wear which here we call 'agwada'. He loaded one of our locally made guns of about 80 cm in length and was getting ready to fire it. Unfortunately for him, a pointed metal on the gun very close to the trigger got hooked in the right pocket of his 'agwada' as he tried to lift it up. On trying to remove it, he unconsciously turned the mouth of the gun to his head and accidentally blew his own brains out," I explained.

My last sentence made his blood freeze. I could see him hold his own head with both hands. I guess the image of blown up brains made him imagine himself in the same situation. He rocked uneasily in his seat.

"Do you now see why the governor banned such an activity in town?" I asked.

No response came from Pa. Instead he turned all his attention to the traditional dance group performing in front of us, headed by Paul's elder brother. I guess he wanted to dispel the images of the horrible picture I painted by concentrating on the traditional dance. I left him alone. However, the traditional dancers performed for 20 minutes and left the arena. It was Paul's turn to take the stage with his own dance group. During the course of their performance, some of the mourners or spectators who admired the performers ran on stage with bank notes in their hands to motivate them. The motivation energized the performers even more and they gave in their utmost best to satisfy the crowd. Their time on stage soon elapsed and they had to make way for the next group. Paul led them to the house of the neighbour where he had kept resources to entertain them with. They were served with porridge plantains as well as rice and stew. There was also a jug of palm wine for them to drink. Paul wanted to give them a special treat. So, he went round asking everyone present in that sitting room their choice of drink. I sat near the door next to a man who must have been in his early 70s who whispered to me that Paul's idea of taking everyone's choice of drink was not a good one. He suggested that what Paul should have done was get drinks in the 32cl bottles in a few crates and let the guests make do

171

with what was available. He added that the 65cl medium size bottles were too expensive and that Paul was not going to cope with the expenses. He further suggested that Paul go in for 'Makosa', a drink brewed and bottled in Nigeria with 45% alcoholic content. It was sweet but could knock someone off pretty fast especially one who was not used to drinking. Besides, it was cheap and could be used to control the appetite of some mourners who came along with nothing but had a wild appetite for alcoholic drinks.

I called Paul outside and whispered the old man's suggestions to him and he bought the ideas. He immediately sent me to get two crates. The dance group was well entertained and they soon made way for the other' guests. Men and women came in. Some of the women carried baskets of food while some of the men brought palm wine. They were served with food and some of the remaining drinks. While they were eating, a man of about 60 years walked in. He came with nothing and seemed to know Paul quite well. He had only his traditional cup made from the horn of a cow.

"I greet you all", he said as he entered the house.

"Thank you Massa Mimbo", some in the house replied. That was how I got to know his name though I was certain it was not his real name. He walked straight to an empty seat and threw himself into it.

"Paul, son of Fru", he called out at the top of his voice as if Paul was far away from him. "Yes Pa Mimbo, welcome", Paul replied. "How is…?"

He did not allow Paul to complete the question.

"How is what? Since you started working in town, what have you done for us back here in the village?" he asked.

172

"Ahh- ahh Pa Mimbo, I am still preparing to come and greet you, my fathers here. I have not forgotten that I am your son", Paul tried to explain.

"Leave all that explanation and bring some two bottles of Big Guinness here for me to clear my eyes with", he said.

All those present in that sitting room started walking out. I really couldn't tell if they were irritated by Pa Mimbo's request or if they were attracted by the performance out at Paul's family compound. All left except four, Paul, Pa Mimbo, the old Man who cautioned us on the types of drinks to buy and me.

"Pa Mimbo, let me offer you this sweet wine so that you can wet your throat with while I go for the Guinness", Paul pleaded.

"Ok my son", he agreed accepting the glass of Makossa that Paul was extending to him. He took a sip and then a second.

"This thing is very sweet," he said.

That was something which he should have taken gradually but since it was sweet and he wanted to take more before other people came in, he quickly emptied the first glass and placed it on the table to be refilled. It was done and he still emptied it in a flash. He still expected it to be refilled but Paul decided to pour only half a glass.

" Fill it up," Pa Mimbo insisted.

Paul asked him to empty the glass first. He did and placed the empty glass again on the table for Paul to refill. Paul did not refill the glass. Pa Mimbo was not happy with the delay and became furious.

"Why don't you want to pour that wine?" he asked. "Don't you know that an event like this offers us the only opportunity to eat all the good things we call luxurious in this village?"

Paul tried to plead with him to rest for a while before having more. But he was too impatient.

"Do you think you have anything here? I learned that Pa Nuncham who lives not too far away from here is very sick and will soon die. Just wait let it happen and you will see something. All his children out of this country would bring all the nice things in this world for us to enjoy. Look at you, only common wine and you cannot pour for people to drink to their satisfaction," Pa Mimbo said mockingly and tried to rise from his seat.

I held my breath as I imagined that his system was not at all used to liquors with high alcoholic contents. He fell back in his seat even after a third attempt. My heart was pounding in my chest as I feared the worse.

"What is happening to me?" he thundered. "What have you given me?"

His actions provoked some laughter in the house. Paul tried to provide and answer but soon discovered that Pa Mimbo was not listening to him as he fell fast asleep. One woman who must have been in her mid 40s walked in and saw Pa Mimbo very helpless. My friend referred to her as Mrs. Celestine. She must have seen him as he rose and fell for the last time and felt that he must have been poisoned. She wailed with all her strength and it drew the attention of some mourners who were outside. Even those who heard from Paul's family compound came rushing in. Among them was Mr. Kombi. He was Pa Mimbo's intimate friend as I was told. They spent most of their time in beer parlours. He did not bother to ask what the matter was or what happened. He immediately whisked his friend away and everything went back to normal. I told my friend after that incident that it was risky serving more than two glasses to any villager who came in, given the high alcoholic content. Trying to curb cost did not mean that we had to kill people.

However, assisting my friend in serving people was enjoyable but not as enjoyable as taking a tour round the village. I told my friend that I wanted to go and see what his village had to offer strangers like me. He regretted the fact that he could not come with me at that moment given that he had to wait and serve guests who came there for him but promised to do so after the death celebration of his father. We separated on that promise.

I went to his family compound to see how things were going. People were moving in and out of the compound and the celebrations were punctuated by traditional dances and gun firing. I hated the sounds of the guns and decided to hurry out to avoid them.

I stepped out of the compound and discovered that the small market outside had grown larger. I think some of the traders simply transferred their small stores to that area outside Paul's family compound. '*When calamity strikes, it makes some people miserable and others happy. What a life,*' I thought to myself. I got on a motor bike and asked the rider to take me round the village. Austin as he was called was more than happy to do it not because he was going to make money but because he enjoyed interacting with someone from town. It was a source of pride. He asked me so many questions about life in town and on the lives of youth especially young girls. He got really excited with the responses I provided especially if there were any similarities with life in the village. Our ride together was going to be short lived as we got to the village square and saw a convoy of vehicles heading to a compound just about 700 meters from there towards the western side of the village. I asked Austin to halt and let the convoy carry on as a lot of dust was raised. I had no intention of returning to town with running nostrils. What I noticed was that there was a picture of a young man posted on the wheel screen of each car in the convoy. The third car which was a Nissan Laurel with 'Last Journey to Heaven' clearly written on it bore the casket. Looking at the picture closely, I considered the late guy too young to be dead. I got curious and decided to forgo my pleasure trip around the village and asked Austin to take me to the yard the hearse drove into. We got there just when the casket was being taken out of the hearse to be laid in front of the house in a special tent which was well decorated for the purpose. Written on the walls of the tent were different messages on cardboard papers. Some of them read; "We love you but God loves you more, The Angels Are Here To Take You Home, Safe journey Home." From what I gathered the late guy was the only one who had studied up to post graduate level in his whole family. His immediate family members had problems holding themselves together as some rolled on the ground while others bent over him as though they wanted to whisper something into his ears. I went closer to the casket to pay my last respects as well. There was an old woman there who wept more than the rest of the mourners and constantly called the name Joshua. I then knew that was the name of the late guy.

As I walked round the casket I noticed that the face of late Joshua had all sorts of bruises as though he was seriously beaten before he died. The bruises might have equally been a result of a motor bike accident but that did not cross my mind then. I had to confirm my suspicion and after paying my respects, I found a corner where mostly youths were. I knew that they would have information on the reason behind Joshua's death. Indeed, they had what I was looking for. I gathered from their conversation that Joshua left the university campus when it was already dark and was heading back to his home when a heavy downpour began unannounced. He decided to hide from the rain on the veranda of someone's house. The owner of the house was inside with his family and locked the door. Joshua did not want to disturb them. So he decided to stay outside the man's house waiting for the rain to subside. The rain started giving way when the man came out and saw Joshua on his veranda and immediately thought of the worse. He thought that Joshua was a thief attempting to take advantage of the heavy rain to rob his house. Most armed robbers especially in the city took advantage of heavy rains to break into homes. Without seeking to know what Joshua was doing there, he immediately raised an alarm that there was a thief around preparing to rob him. Neighbours came out and just started kicking and beating him with any weapon they could lay hands on. One of his school mates recognized him but before he could call the mob to reason, it was already too late for Joshua. He died of both internal and external wounds on the way to the hospital. He was just another victim of a social system which had broken down. I sought to know from them if they had any idea of what became of the 'whistle blower' when he discovered that through his fault an innocent student was killed. One of them who claimed to have been at the capital city at the time said the 'whistle blower' was a well to do man and with the help of some men in high places, he was arrested and released shortly afterwards. They considered that it was just a mistake. That was how porous the justice system was. Anyone who had the money could buy his freedom. A poor boy who stole a loaf of bread out of hunger had to face the full weight of the law…. That law that was very selective.

My desire to discover the village was killed by what I learned happened to Joshua. The money spent and the energy deployed by his parents went in vain. I could feel their pain and could not blame them if they felt anger against the whistle blower and the regime in place. I left the place and went back to the neighbour's house where Paul was entertaining his guests. He was the only one there and it became obvious that no one was going to come there for him. We then left for their family compound to watch some traditional dance groups who were still performing. I told him of what I saw as I went out and he felt terrible because he knew the late guy perfectly well. But he could not go there at that moment because he was tired.

"I have played my part and what is left is the family meeting tomorrow. I want to go and rest for about three hours and after that we shall go to Joshua's funeral," he said and left for his room while I remained outside watching the dance groups perform.

17

At 21:00 we put on warm clothes and moved to Joshua's funeral. There was a lot of music and the mourners danced to its rhythm in a large circle. The music was played by Loh Benson, a renowned artist who performed at most funerals in the province. Over the years, he trained many young men who equally took up the trade. As he was growing older, mostly the young men he trained went out to entertain at funerals. But there were some he insisted on being there in person and Joshua' was one of them. His songs ranged from religious to social satire. One of his hit songs touched many and moved a good number to tears. As it went on, majority of the mourners moved back to their seats. The song went thus...

When I was sick, very sick,
Slept in the hospital,
Nobody came,
Now that I'm dead,
People have come,
But there're no eyes to see them

When I was sick, very sick
Food to eat there wasn't
Now that I'm dead
Rice has come
But there isn't mouth to eat it

When I was sick, very sick
Water to drink there wasn't

Now that I'm dead whisky has come
But there is no mouth to drink it.

When I was sick, very sick
Someone to talk to, there wasn't
But now that I'm dead
People have come
But there's no mouth to talk to them

If you have any food to give
Let me have my share now
'Cause
Tomorrow
Tomorrow
Tomorrow
Might be late.

If you have any drinks to offer
Let me have my share now
'Cause
Tomorrow
Tomorrow
Tomorrow
Might be late.

If you have anything to do for me
Better do it now that I'm still alive
'Cause
Tomorrow
Tomorrow
Tomorrow
Might be late.

He was to perform the whole night. It attracted many mourners and it seemed the whole village converged there. Paul and I were definitely not going to spend the night there after a long and tiring day. We left the premises at 02:30 and got a bike which took us back to their family compound. With dizziness which was already at its peak, we had no problem falling asleep. We badly needed it after working all day.

We woke up the next morning at 09:50 and moved to the sitting room. It was already full with Paul's brothers and sisters as well as uncles, aunts and cousins. They were discussing how the land property left behind by Late Mr. Fru Jones was going to be shared without problems and also who was going to be the late man's successor. Paul was very surprised to see that discussions were already going on and nobody bothered to come and alert him in his room. He did not stop there to ask why just then but went out to clean his mouth and face. I went with him and we returned at the same time. As he entered the sitting room where his whole family was assembled, I remained outside. I sat on the bench that was against the wall, very close to the window. From there, I could hear everything that was being said inside the house.

My friend did not want the discussions to go without having answers to the kind of treatment he was getting after the death of his father till that moment. He started by acknowledging the presence of his uncles and aunts as well as cousins. After thanking them for making the death celebration successful, he went straight to what was bothering him.

"For some time now, there has been a kind of negative attitude towards me and I don't understand why. First, it was information of the death of papa which was kept from me and I got here only to learn that he had been buried. I did not set my eyes on the corpse of the man who gave me life before he was buried. This morning, the family meeting had begun and no one had bothered to come and inform me. I want to have explanations," he said.

It was his elder brother Fredrick who attempted to give him answers. He sounded rather hostile and sarcastic in the way he began.

"Your wife whom you treat as an egg is heavily pregnant and I thought that there was no need informing you of papa's death. That would have pushed you to abandon your precious wife to come here whereas you would not have done anything to change papa's situation," he said.

"What is that supposed to mean?" Paul asked.

"What I am telling you is that you do not belong to this family and you should count yourself lucky that we've allowed you to be up here even now," Fredrick said.

It was becoming a bitter exchange between Paul and his elder brother. One of their uncles who was there decided to step in and regain some order.

"If you have forgotten your manners, your parents who are elderly and present here are supposed to make you reason before speaking. My brother has hardly made two days in the land of his ancestors and his sons are already talking as bitter enemies. His body must be turning in the grave now. If the two of you do not have the same father, you at least have the same mother. That means that you are still brothers and are supposed to be looking in the same direction," he said.

That certainly confused my friend even more as the speakers were not clear. I would have felt the same way if I

182

was in my friend's shoes. And so he decided to turn to his mother.

"Mother, Fredrick said a while ago that I do not belong to this family. Uncle Tom has just said that even if Fredrick and I do not have the same father, we at least have the same mother. I think you are the one who can clear all this up. What is going on mother? What are they talking about?" Paul asked.

I could hear someone sobbing and I was certain that it was his mother. The crying intensified as Paul told her that the tears were not giving him the answers he badly wanted to hear. But there was no word from her and it was Fredrick who took the floor again.

"I think the time has come for us to put an end to this silly secret we have been keeping in this family. I know it will be a shock to many of you in here. But believe me, it was not easy for any of us when it happened. Paul, Sophia is my immediate follower and do you know the age gap between us," he asked.

"I know that you two have almost four years between you. But where is this age gap leading us to? I wanted to know why I have been sidelined in matters that concern the family of late. In response, you started talking about me not belonging to this family and it soon moved to us not having the same father and now you are talking about age gap. What is the connection?

"Don't be in a hurry, you will soon know," Fredrick said. "What is the age gap between Sophia and you?"

"It is less than two years," Paul replied.

"Have you ever bothered to ask yourself why?" Fredrick asked.

"I must admit that I have never bothered to ask myself why because I know that a child could come earlier than the parents expected…I wouldn't want to call it a love accident," Paul said.

"There you are right," Fredrick went on. "But that was not the case in your situation. What happened was that less than ten months after Sophia was born, my mother went to the farm one Thursday and when returning home after working all day, she was attacked by someone she did not know. The man did not only attack her but he raped her as well. You are the product of that unholy act and that is why I said a while ago that you are not a member of this family."

I was not in the house to see the look on the face of my friend and could only imagine myself in his place. Information like that one which was unleashed in a gathering would have made me jump. It would not have surprised me if he decided to make a very drastic decision after that.

"Is it true mother?" Paul asked almost in tears.

"Yes my son," she said sobbing.

"How come nobody has ever talked to me about it?" Paul asked.

"My father never wanted us to breathe anything about it to anyone. Do you know what my mother would have become if that kind of story ever got out? She would have been treated like a prostitute or an outcast though what happened to her was through no fault of hers. Father too would have lost respect and he really fought hard as a man to do what no other man would have done in such a situation. I don't need to tell you what stigmatization can do. It took him six years to accept my mother again as a wife. He felt really hurt in his pride and needed to convince himself that what happened to his wife was not her fault. Six years happens to be the age gap between you and Emily, your immediate follower. So don't go thinking that it was because my mother had problems falling pregnant after you were born. He adopted you and treated you like his own child," Fredrick said.

"That makes everything clear now. I guess there is no need asking why I was not called when this meeting started. I have now been brandished a stranger because the man I've known all my life as a father is no longer here. I think the real reason why you are treating me like this is still to come," Paul said.

"Two weeks before your father got really sick and eventually died, he expressed his wish that Paul be made his successor when he is gone. He also wanted Paul to be the one to share all that has been left behind because he is educated and stands a better chance to understand the needs of everyone in here," Paul's mother said.

"I can't believe you told him that. You still want him to continue receiving the preferential treatment even after the death my father? He went to the best school and has been lucky to have a government job. What do I have? He is not the son of my father yet he is the one chosen to succeed him. What about us the legitimate children of my father?" Fredrick asked.

"My husband was a very good man and I will not allow you to start questioning the way he did things. You were all treated the same way. You were both sent to the same school but you were stubborn and preferred having things the easy way. That was what kept you out of school. Even after doing everything to get you back in school, you deliberately refused to go. You are now accusing your father of giving your brother preferential treatment. Please, just let my husband rest in peace," Paul's mother said sobbing intensely.

"I hate him because he was always doing things to please my father. That made my father prefer him over me. I can't believe that there is someone in here who is going to support that the son of a stranger be made the successor of Mr. Fru Jones," Fredrick said.

"When it came to making contributions intended for the well-being of the family, I gave the lion's share and back then, I was not considered a stranger. When you were sick, you called me and asked for my assistance. I did not hesitate even for a second. You did not consider the help coming from a stranger. You seem to forget that I am the one paying the fees of little Theresa, your fourth child and you do not consider the assistance coming from a stranger. Now that it has come to succession and the sharing of property I'm considered a stranger. If it is going to make you happy, I am not interested. I have a house in the city of my own and do not see how I could abandon it to come here and be a successor. You can have it and do what you want with it. I only pray that it makes you responsible. Before I go, I have only one request to make and it is that you should never call my number again," Paul said and got out of the house.

I followed him and asked where he was going. His response was rigid and authoritative.

"Go and get your things ready because we are leaving right away," he said.

I did not ask any further questions and went to his room where we spent the night and put his things as well as mine together. He soon came to the room and carried his little box while I carried mine. We passed through the sitting room where there was dead silence and all eyes were on us. Tears

186

were streaming down the eyes of Paul's mother and I guessed that she was not happy with the cracks within her family just days after the death of her husband. Paul told her in the hearing of everyone that he was going to send for her in the days ahead. We left Paul's family compound without saying goodbye to his brothers and sisters. Separation in anger especially with loved ones was not good as one could not tell whether it was the last separation or not. I could not tell him to go and say goodbye to them because I knew perfectly well why he was angry with them. Apart from his uncle and mother, no one else stood up to utter a word in his favour or support him. I was tempted to believe that they were all in alliance with their elder brother and just had to stand by him no matter the decision he took.

At 12:05, we were on board a Toyota Coaster bus bound for the city of Bamenda. It was very scanty given that there were not many passengers in it. That was not good as it meant that we were going to have many stops on the way as the driver was definitely going to be picking up and dropping passengers most of the time. The few passengers who were in the bus were mostly in front and my friend and I moved to the back seat where we could converse freely.

"I know that because of greed, your father's last wish is going to be ignored," I said.

"That is not something new. What makes me angry is that my elder brother's attitude of having things the easy way has not gone away. As for being my father's successor, that does not bother me. I would have declined anyway. That thing is some kind of prison and I have no intention of locking myself in it. My brother is fighting to be the successor thinking that it is going to be as easy as he imagines. He will be very shocked. After all, he and the rest of them there are the ones still struggling to find their feet. I am already settled and don't see what I should be fighting back there with them for," he said.

"Why did Fredrick keep talking about your wife in a sarcastic tone?" I asked.

"That should not surprise you. He has always loved to have things the easy way without toiling for them. All left to him, I would have been surrendering a quarter of what I make every month to him. That was possible when I was not married but he has refused to understand that I now have a family and they have to be my first priority. He sees my wife as the one who is preventing me from giving him the money he wants. That is why I have decided to build my house in the city. If I were to build it here and something happened to me, I'm sure they would kick my wife and children out and keep the house. But there in the city, there are people who would fight for my family. It would not surprise me if they share everything or my brother confiscates a greater part of the property and leaves my mother out. That is why I told my mother that I would send for her in the days ahead," he explained.

"I know that your brother is greedy but I don't think that he would be greedy to the extent of taking away everything including that which is supposed to be meant for his own mother," I said.

My friend was alarmed at my remarks and the expression on his face said everything. He was definitely asking himself if we both lived on the same planet.

"I don't seem to know why that should surprise you. There are a good number of women who are advanced in age and are living in the streets there in the city. Some of them carry trays of groundnuts or oranges on their heads to move

188

around and sell in order to have something to keep life going. You see them every day. Do you think they don't have children? They do but a good number of such children are like my brother who would take away everything including what is meant for their mothers. That aside, do you know how many children my brother has? He has eight children with different women. The sad thing is that he has refused to recognize some of them and does not take care of any. Then why is he fighting for property? It is just to squander it and it will not surprise me if he sells our family compound which my mother is supposed to live in. Do you still have doubts that he is capable of doing such a thing?" he asked.

"Such an act would be the peak of ingratitude and it is better if children who treat their mothers in such a way were never born," said.

A long silence ensued after I said that. I turned my attention to the sceneries on both sides of the road. They were green and beautiful. The bus soon grinned to a halt. The driver wanted to pick up a passenger who was heading to the city. We all had our attention on the passenger who was to join us in the bus. Since he had no luggage, there was no time to waste and we were on the move again as soon as he was seated. I soon took a little bottle of fruit juice that I bought before we boarded the bus and started drinking. Just then some words came out of Paul's mouth which I least expected. I almost choked on the juice.

"I will look for time and come back to the village to look for my biological father," he said.

"Did I hear you well? You will look for time to go back to the village to look for whom? Did you say your biological father?" I asked

He did not say anything.

189

" What is a father to you? Is it the one that went enjoying himself and you came? Or the one who raised you?" I asked.

There was still no response and I went on.

"Are you trying to let me know that late Mr. Fru Jones was just a caretaker? He took care of you from the moment you were born, sent you to school, provided a roof over your head, took you to the hospital when you were sick, carried you on his back when you could not cross the river, put a loaf of bread in your bag when you were going to school and to crown it all, he wanted you to be his successor in his last wish before he left this world. What else do you want? Was that not being father enough to you? What do you need a father for now by the way? Are you sure that the one you plan to go and look for would have done what that late man did for you knowing full well that he was not your biological father? Truly, the man you intend going to look for is your biological father because he is the one who raped your mother. But If I were you, I would not even bother because, he raped your mother before you came. Rape is a crime and anyone who carries out the act is not out to make children but to satisfy his bestial instincts. So, even if you found him, I'm not sure that, he will recognize you. By the way, your mother does not know the man. Are you sure that he was from your village? Where do you intend to go and begin the search? Science has come with DNA. Are you going to have your whole village and neighbouring villages tested? My friend, hearing you say that you're going to look for someone simply because he is your biological father is the most insane thing that has ever come out of your mouth," I said.

He still remained silent like a tomb and I began to imagine that perhaps he was not serious about it and just wanted to see my reaction. Finally he said that he had heard

190

everything I said. That rested the topic. We soon got to the city late in the afternoon and boarded separate taxis to our different homes.

18

On Tuesday 5th August at 08:30, which was barely 48 hours after we returned from Paul's village, he called and informed me that his wife started having some contractions and they were on their way to the Bamenda Regional Hospital. I told him that I was going to meet them at the hospital as soon as I could. Helen was not at my house when he called and so, I called her to let her know where I was going. I left for the hospital after having a bath and taking my breakfast. At 09:15, I was not at the main gate into the hospital premises but at the minor gate that led directly to the maternity ward and the labour room. Vehicles could not get into the hospital premises through that minor gate given its narrow nature. There was a gateman who checked what everyone leaving the hospital through that gate carried. He checked most importantly consultation books because some patients came to the hospital and left without settling their bills. I could not blame the hospital staff for keeping someone at the gates.

That notwithstanding, I got to the section of the labour room reserved for loved ones and guests and found my friend there. He looked very nervous and I understood why. Giving life was a matter of life and death and the rate of mothers who died while giving birth was still high. One was never too sure of what was going to happen. I tried to console my friend by telling him that all was going to be well as God was in control. I knew my turn was to come some day and he would certainly have to console me as well.

After three hours of waiting, a midwife soon emerged from the labour room and told my friend that they came to the hospital a bit too early and that was why his wife was delaying in offloading. But she added that they were going to induce her labour if it took much longer. My friend told her that she was the expert and should do everything to ensure that his wife was ok as well as the baby. She told him not to worry because his wife was in good hands. She said all that with a smile on her face. That too was very reassuring. She left us and went back to the labour room.

My friend's nervousness was still there and I knew that it was going to go away only after he saw his wife and child. I asked him to take a walk with me around the hospital premises. I was certain that it would take away some of his anxiety at least for a while. We went right to the little gate and decided to make a u-turn. As we got closer to the labour room again, we saw the midwife who was to ensure the safe delivery of my friend's wife. She was looking for my friend. I was supposed to leave them talk privately but I went there to hear whatever she wanted to say.

"The items you brought to be used in the delivery of your wife are not enough," she said.

"My wife started coming to this hospital for check up and lectures since she was five months pregnant. The list of items needed for her delivery was given to her here. I bought everything that was on the list. I don't understand how you can tell me now that they are not enough. What is lacking?" my friend asked.

"There are some of the items that you were supposed to buy two or three but you bought just one. You know that it is better that things should be in excess than they be in shortage. I have some of the things that are lacking in there. You could just give me the money and I will supplement," she said.

"How much will the extra items cost," Paul asked.

"They would cost 10.000 Frs." she replied.

Paul immediately pulled the money from his pocket and gave it to her. She rushed back into the labour room with a smile on her face. I was staring at him and he could probably read what was on my mind.

"I know what I have just done there is crazy. The extra items or drugs she says she has in that labour room are probably the leftover of some other women she is now selling to me. That is if at all the items are indeed there. Yet there are notices all over the place that no medical personnel should be involved in the selling of drugs or items within the hospital premises. But what penalties are there for defaulters? Those notices have been there for more than four years now. It would appear those who wrote and signed the notices just wanted to give the impression that they were doing something about the exploitation and business in this hospital. That 10,000 francs I gave her is twice the amount I used to buy all the items my wife needed for her delivery," he said with a sigh.

"If you were aware of the notices forbidding her from selling drugs in the hospital premises, why did you give her the money then?" I asked.

"Smith if you were not my friend, I would have given you the kick of the year," he said. "Your questions are sometimes annoying. You sound sometimes as though you are not living in this city. Many women have come here to give birth and have ended up dying, some with their babies. Why do you think we still have a high rate of mothers dying while giving birth? Midwives are contributing to that high rate. When she says that some items are lacking and she has them to sell, just give her the money. If you don't she might decide to neglect your wife and she will die with her baby. Do you think I gave her the money because I did not know that she was lying? I was buying the life of my wife and that of my baby with that money," he said almost in tears.

"I am sorry…..please wipe your eyes…I shouldn't have asked that stupid question," I said.

I apologized not because I felt that my question was stupid but because I knew he was under intense pressure and needed something to make it lighter for him. I was however convinced that he was on the one hand promoting an illegal business by giving money to the midwife but on the other hand, I felt that he really did not have a choice. The presence of alternatives was supposed to make life easier but it was not the case in my friend's situation. I think I would have done the same thing if I found myself in the same situation. In a society where laws were passed but remained only on paper, things were bound to be that way. But my friend had a revelation which was shocking to me.

"The level of corruption in this country stinks right up to the high heavens," he said. "That is why God has turned his face from us and things can no longer work normally again. I have never revealed this to anyone. Some three years ago I was awarded a contract to supply computers to one of the government high schools here in town. He who awarded me the contract did so with some strings attached. I had to surrender 10% of the contract money to him. He who had to sign for the funds to be disbursed to me had his own percentage. The cashier who had to give me the physical cash had his own percentage. The government that gave me the money to do the work held back 20% as tax. At the end of the day, I was left with very little and forced to review my initial plans. What I supplied were second-handed Pentium two outdated computers instead of the Pentium three brand new computers I initially planned on supplying. That was not even the most annoying part of it. If you saw the lavish ceremony that was organized to receive the outdated computers, you would have wept. The so-called big people were dressed in expensive Italian three piece suits looking like gentlemen when in reality they were thieves. That is not all; look at the amount of money the international community pumps into this country for the fight against the spread of HIV-AIDS. Do you know that I heard on BBC that more than two-third of that money was swallowed up by corruption? NGOs which exist only on paper in brief cases are created every now and then to lobby for funds to fight against HIV-AIDS. Free generic drugs which are given to be handed to AIDS sufferers free of charge end up in private drug stores. That is why I have no respect for those in authority in this country or anyone that joins them," he said with a sigh.

"Wait a minute, there is something I don't understand. The government gives you money to supply computers to a government school and you have to surrender 20% of the amount given to you back to that same government. Why did it not deduct the 20% at once and then give you the amount it wanted you to supply the computers with?" I asked.

"Listen my friend, you seem not to understand anything. What happens is that the government would earmark 100 million for the supply of computers. It would go on National Radio and Television and announce it there. After announcing it, it calls for me the contractor who has won the contract after promising a percentage to the jury which studied my file to come and sign documents. I would sign that I received 100 million francs for the contract. The 100 million would get out of the state coffers but it would not be handed to me. An agent who would claim to be a government agent would come and say 20% of the 100 million will be held back as tax. That 20% does not go back to the state coffers," he explained.

"Where does the 20% go to?" I asked.

"Where does the billions earmarked for projects which never see the light of day go to?" he responded.

"I guess there is no need asking why the government would tax an amount it gives you to carry a project on its behalf," right?

"You have started understanding. After the 20% that is held back, other percentages have to follow and at the end of the day, what I have to carry out the project is less than half the amount announced on state radio and television. That is the system. You would have expected just as any common man on the street that any project on behalf of the government should be tax free but that is not the case. It is the system as I've just said and those at the top are very desperate to keep it that way. You see, education is a very relative term and unfortunately the education received by those who govern us is inadequate and can only be described as such. That is why they are so scared of those who possess that power called knowledge. Do you know why you teachers cannot have the extra money you keep requesting from the government? It is because they are afraid that more money in your hands would make you powerful and with that power, you could topple this system that they are benefiting from. What can you therefore do against such a powerful force? Sometimes you have to get into it to survive. I have to bribe and corrupt in order to survive because the system has made it too hard to do things otherwise," he said with a sigh.

198

My mind was clouded and buried in desperation and I did not know what else to say. However, thirty minutes after the midwife took the money from my friend and went back to the labour room, she came out again with a fixed smile on her face. That was an indication that there was no need for us to panic. She broke the news we wanted to hear as soon as she got to where I and my friend stood.

"Congratulations sir, your wife has been delivered of a bouncing baby boy. Mother and child are doing fine," she said.

My friend breathed a sigh of relief and asked if he could see his family. The nurse replied that they were still cleaning mother and child up and my friend had to wait for a little while. She further asked my friend to celebrate while waiting for his wife and child.

"I am doing that by hugging my friend here," he said.

"You can do more than that by throwing a round of drinks for those of us who made things work well," she said.

The smile that the news of the successful delivery brought to my face dried up. I wanted to ask her if the 10,000 Frs. that was given to her was not enough but gave up the idea after a second thought. My friend was also not happy with what she said but was careful not to let her know that he was hurt. He simply told her that he was going to organize a special celebration and invite her personally. With those words, she went back to the labour room to continue her work while we remained outside waiting.

She finally came out of the labour room twenty minutes after the announcement by the midwife. The midwife who brought the news supported her while another midwife carried the baby. I took the baby from her while my friend helped to support his wife to the maternity ward. Since it was a male child, they had to spend at least four days in the hospital and leave after the child was circumcised. I spent some time in the maternity ward my friend's wife was taken to, admiring the baby. I called Helen to alert her of the marvellous event. I equally pleaded with her to get over to the house and prepare some food to bring to the hospital for my friend's wife. She asked me to come to the house so that we could do the cooking together and also added that she had something really important to tell me. We promised to meet at my house some 30 minutes from then.

I did not leave in 30 minutes as I promised Helen. I left an hour later because I just could not take my eyes off my friend's baby. I kept asking myself when I would carry one of my own in my arms. I was working and what was still preventing me from having one was indecision and procrastination. Whatever the case, I knew I had to make the decision sooner or later because I could not go on procrastinating all my life. However, I arrived home at 13:40 and Helen was there already doing the cooking. She reminded me that I was half an hour late and I apologized. That was to avoid further questions that might have led to a confrontation. Without wasting too much time, I asked her what she had to tell me that was so important. She smiled and then took out a piece of paper from her handbag which she handed to me.

"What is this?" I asked.

"It is in your hands. Take a look and stop asking questions," she said.

It was a pregnancy test result with her name on it. It was positive. My knees got weak and I sunk into the chair that was behind me. That was something a dreamt of barely an hour earlier but getting the news that I was going to be a father not long from then was too much for me. Helen certainly expected that I was going to leap with joy but my behaviour after seeing her positive pregnancy results made her worried and confused.

"What darling? Aren't you happy about it?" she asked.

"Of course I am," I replied with tears spilling out of my eyes. "Thank you for making me a father."

"Come with me to the kitchen so that we can do things faster. The wife of your friend might start feeling hungry," she said.

"Ok, I will be right behind you," I said.

We went to the kitchen and she gave me tomatoes and onions to slice. When I was through, she gave me some other little ingredients to grind on a grinding stone. She was always happy when I assisted her in doing one or two things in the kitchen. Though I was doing what she wanted, my mind was concentrated on what lay ahead. Her test results put an end to my procrastination and indecision but raised other worries. I lived in a society with people who had problems minding their own business. The way people lived their lives and what people did or did not do spiced most gossips. I did not want people to hang the status of a bastard or illegitimacy on my child. So I planned to legalize things between Helen and I in the shortest possible time before her stomach started protruding. I did not want to give the gossipers something to spice their gossips with. We both left for the hospital and got there at 14:40. When my friend and his wife had eaten, I broke the news of Helen's pregnancy to them.

"Well brother that is wonderful news. Welcome to the club of parenthood. I'm sure that will put an end to bachelorhood," he said.

201

I told him that bachelorhood was something I had to do away with as soon as possible. He wanted to know how soon and I said that before school reopened for the new academic year. That was less than a month away. Organizing a traditional as well as a court wedding when schools had already reopened was going to be difficult as I was supposed to grapple with the school workload. It was therefore imperative that I made use of the short time I still had ahead of me.

I went out of the ward and had a little chat with my father on the phone. I told him of what I wanted to do and within the shortest possible time. He called it a miracle because he had long expected it and as it wasn't forthcoming so he gave up after some time. I asked him if it did not bother him where the girl came from.

"How she looks or where she comes from does not matter to me. All I need to know is that the person you want to marry can wear a skirt or gown and can have children," he said.

He promised to come over to the city 48 hours later for us to move to the home of my future father-in-law to find out all that was needed to legally take Helen as a wife. Her parents as well as a good number of her family members were in the city. But I did not know if her father was going to rally his relatives for the traditional rites to be done in the city or if he was going to insist that we go and do things in his village. He came from the same village as my friend William and the thought of facing the bad road made my blood freeze. I prayed hard that he made the exception of letting us do things in the city. More so, that was not my only preoccupation. I wondered if he was going to ask me to go and come after two weeks as tradition demanded. If that were to be the case, things were definitely going to extend to the school period and I did not want that to happen because I did not want anything interfering with my school work.

Helen and I spent quite some time with my friend and his wife. A good number of their family members started arriving at the hospital. Since they had company, I felt that it was time for Helen and I to go and handle our own business. I pleaded with her to go and plead with her father to convince his other family members to let us do all the traditional rites in the city. She guaranteed that she was going to convince him and I told her of the arrival of my father not long from then. We arrived my house at 17:30 and she made food for me and left for their family home soon after.

The next morning, Helen called me at 08:05 from the hospital to know of my whereabouts. I told her that I was at home and asked her what she was doing in the hospital. She told me that she was there to give my friend's wife some breakfast but went on to ask why I wanted to know what she was doing at the hospital. I told her that I was worried there might have been a reason other than my friend's wife. She then told me that she was on her way to the house.

At 09:05 she walked into the house as the main door was open. I asked her how my friend's wife and the baby were doing and she responded that they were all doing fine. I then asked her if she had spoken to her father. She said that she did and he had no problem with the traditional wedding rites holding in the city. The only inconvenience was that some of her paternal relatives had to be called in from the village. Lucky enough, Helen told me that they had communicated with them already and they were definitely going to be arriving to the city later that afternoon. She was not supposed to spend the night at my house given that she and her family were going to receive some important guests the next day. For that reason, she left before midday for their home to go and help make preparations. I watched TV and at about 15:00, I went to the hospital to spend some time with my friend and his wife. I stayed with them until 19:00 when I decided to go back home.

On Thursday 07th August at 07:20, I heard a knock on my door. I opened it and behold it was my father, Mr. Smith William. He was not alone. He came with his brother, Uncle Joe. I knew my uncle was going to say something.

"At last, you have decided to be a man and keep aside your skirt," he said.

"I am not a woman and have never owned a skirt," I retorted.

"You must not own a skirt or put one on to be a woman. Somebody who wears trousers but cannot make a firm decision, or is fond of procrastinating or runs away when a problem is coming is not a man. We call such men women in trousers. Now that you've decided to hang your skirt, I can only be happy. I only hope you will not turn my house into a hideout when you have your differences," he said laughing.

"Now I know that it is only my own family member that can ridicule me," I said.

"Please son, I am not the enemy here. I've come here to encourage and give you my blessings as well as my unconditional support as you step into that new school call marriage. Yes son, it is a new school and only the two of you are going to be teachers and learners. Don't go reading things in books to come and apply in your house. You might start a fire which might require the services of fire fighters to put out. There are couples who quarrel and fight. That is their way of expressing their love for each other. After a fight, you are supposed to come out stronger and closer to each other," he said.

"Thank you indeed uncle, I know I can always count on you for support," I said.

Since there wasn't much time, I asked them to move to the dining table and have some breakfast. They did and we left soon after for the house of my future father-in-law.

We arrived at the gate of my future father-in-law at 09:30. It was open and that was an indication that he was expecting me and my family. We walked right into his yard and were ushered into the sitting room where Helen's aunts and uncles as well as cousins were already seated. They all welcomed us with smiles on their faces as we moved to the seats that were reserved for us. Once we were seated, Helen's father rose from his seat and cleared his throat.

"My brothers and sisters, good morning once again and welcome to our guests," he began. "When we get married and give birth to children, we expect them to grow up and become independent some day. Until they become independent, we cannot really say that we have succeeded as parents. We are all gathered here today because we want to happily usher one of our daughters to the new path of independence she has decided to take. Trying to stop her would be tantamount to killing her happiness. I can see that there is a smile on every face in this house and that is a sign that we all love our daughter and care about her happiness. However, I would like to apologize for the modifications we've had to make to the way things are usually done. According to tradition things were supposed to be done only in the village. In addition, our in-laws were supposed to come first for the introduction and leave to return again for the list of items they would present before taking their woman away. After taking the list, they were to go and return only two weeks later with all that was listed on it. That would be what we all call bride price. We are now educated people and I feel that we are not supposed to be slaves to tradition. We should be able to make adjustments for the sake of convenience once in a while. The road to the village is not a good one and we wouldn't want to subject our in-laws to the ordeal of the bad roads. For that reason, our in-laws would be presented with a list of items they would pay as bride price here today and they would go and return in one week instead of two. We have been forced to make these adjustments because of the kind of work our son-in-law does. I think we are still working within tradition."

He decided to take his seat and it was my father who took the floor after him.

"Thank you very much for the adjustments you've made for our sake. I agree with you that we are not supposed to become slaves to tradition. The times are changing and some aspects of tradition that do not correspond to the changing times are supposed to be done away with. We are not in any way saying that we should abandon our tradition. If we do that, we would have lost our identity. That said, we are gathered here today because our children have decided that it is time to leave their brothers and sisters as well as parents to go and form their own family. Their union does not unite only the two of them but their two families as well. Our family has now grown bigger. However, we were walking in a forest of fruit trees and found a beautiful ripe fruit on our path. We knew that the fruit fell from a particular tree. We could not have just picked the fruit and continue on our way without identifying that tree and at least looking at it. We are here not only to look at the tree but also to ask the tree if it can grant us the permission to take one of its fruits away," he said regaining his seat.

It was one of Helen's uncles who spoke next.

"You did well to look for the tree from which the beautiful fruit fell. Many people do not do that today. They just find the fruit, pick it and start eating it without looking at the tree that produced it. That is why the rate of legal marriages is falling while the rate of cohabitation commonly known as "Come we stay" is on the rise these days. We thank you for looking for the tree," he said and took his seat.

Helen's father rose again and said that the ceremony was not to be made only of speeches. He asked that a large flask which was on the dining table at one end of the house be brought to the centre of the sitting room. All of us present in the house had to eat what was in the flask. That was a symbol that both families had became one and the family of Helen had given us permission to take their daughter. Porridge plantain was the food in the flask and it was pushed down throats by the two crates of assorted drinks we brought. People went to the dining table after eating the plantain to have another meal of their choice. There was much to eat and drink.

We did not immediately go back to business after eating. We were allowed to relax for a short while in order to let digestion take place. Plantain was hard food to be eaten in the early hours of the morning. Some cool music was played to accompany the digestion. Sipping of wine and beer formed part of the relaxation. That lasted for some 30 minutes and we went back to business. My father-in-law rose from his seat just as he did when we entered his house some two and a half hours earlier and cleared his throat. Everyone in the house became attentive.

"Our guests here have come to ask the hand of Helen in marriage. When it came to conceiving her, it was the job of just me and my wife. When she was born, she became the child of the community and all of us in here form that community. You have all been invited so that together we can hold the hand of our daughter and usher her onto the new path she has decided to take and to wish her well as she moves on. It is time for us to present the list of items our guests will have to bring one week from today. What kind of list are we going to present to our guests? Is it one that would prove to them that we are trading our daughter as a commodity? Or is it one that will prove to them that our daughter is and will always remain a link between both families? Since Helen is our daughter, I will allow my brother Thomas, to answer that question and also present the list," he said and sat down.

"Thank you my brother for giving me this opportunity and the honour to say something regarding the future of our daughter," Thomas began. "Many young men and women today have decided to cohabit. Somewhere, we cannot really blame them. The greed of some of our parents has pushed them into such cohabitations. You cannot imagine that a young man would get up one fine day to go and ask the hand of a woman he has fallen in love with only to be asked to bring half a million, or a million or two million and sometimes up to three million francs to pay as bride price. When the young man tries to complain, they will try to give some justification. Some would try to justify the high amount by pointing to the education given to the girl as if they gave birth to her expecting someone else to come and take care of her education. Some would try to use the girl's job or physical appearance or the fact that she had been abroad to justify such high amounts charged. The question we ask is that with the high rate of unemployment and the economic crisis that are crushing many young men today, where do such greedy parents expect them to get such amounts of money? The worse thing is that they do not bother to think of the impact of their actions on the young girl they are giving away. When the marriage is no longer working, some of them become prisoners in the home of the young man because her relatives would be unable to refund the bride price already taken and consumed. Marriage today has become one of the most unsafe insinuations one can think of. Would we want to send our daughter into prison in the name of marriage?" he asked.

The response was unanimous. "NO," they all shouted.

"In that case, we should stick to the token our forefathers laid down to be the bride price," Thomas went on. "The paying of the bride price is never over because when there is an occasion in this family or a ceremony, or a problem, our son-in-law will be called upon to do something. That will still be the bride price. We should not go charging millions as a bride price and expect him to still help when there is something to be taken care of in our family. That would not be only greed but also exploitation which in the long run would imprison our daughter. So, as concerns what is on this list, our guests would have to go and come with two bags of salt, a carton of soap, a tin of palm oil and the sum of 50,000 francs. That was the token our forefathers took as bride price and we are not going to depart from it. The day our daughter leaves our son-in-law's house, which we are not wishing for, with the reason that she is being maltreated and comes back here, we will take her in. I'm sure I have spoken the mind of everyone in here."

There was a round of applause as Thomas finished saying what he had to say. My father rose and thanked them for not departing from the amount their fathers agreed on. He went on to express his happiness with becoming one with a family as educated and united as that of my father-in-law. He ended by promising that we were going to be there in one week with the items asked for. We left shortly after we received the list of items and it was 14:05 on my watch. Uncle Joe went back to his house while I went to my house with my father. He stayed for just a short while and then left for the village after promising to return a day before we had to pay the bride price.

The next day which happened to be the third day after Paul's son was born, I went to the hospital to visit them. I got there at 09:30 when the child had just been circumcised. He was crying terribly and his mother was doing all she could to calm him down. I was heartbroken seeing the wound on the baby and my blood chilled as though the wound was on me. I could not bear seeing it and the baby crying and asked my friend to accompany me out of the maternity ward.

While we were outside, I told him everything that transpired when I went to the home of my father-in-law with my father and uncle. I told him of the items they asked and he was very surprise.

"Brother, you are very lucky. I can't believe that they asked you to bring only 50.000 francs in cash. I was not so lucky. I was asked to bring a million francs. The reason that was advanced to justify such an amount was that my wife was educated and beautiful. I got furious and left without taking her. She stayed with her family for some months and left in anger after trying in vain to make them reduce the amount. We went and had our court and church weddings and it was after the birth of our second child that we went back and the amount was reduced to half a million. Even then, it was after she went there and threatened those who were imposing the amount that they were going to take care of her if she lost her husband. She fixed an amount that they would have to provide her each month for her up keep if they caused her husband to leave her and her two children. Since they could not afford it, they were forced to cut down the one million by half. I still have one hundred thousand to go and pay for the bride price to be complete," he explained.

"Did you say complete? The paying of bride price is for life. Do you want to tell me that if there is something in her family that requires some kind of contribution you would not contribute? Of course you will….that will still be the bride price you are paying. By the way, was the one million the only item you had to pay?" I asked.

"It was the last item on a whole catalogue. I always ask myself if people try to fit themselves in the shoes of others before doing things. If they were the ones who were given the list, I'm sure they would have left for good. But since greedy people find it easier to take than to give, they always make excessive demands without thinking. That aside, you have been coming to this hospital and passing only through that little gate. Do you know what has been happening around the main gate of this hospital which is much further from here?" he asked.

"Tell me something I don't know," I said.

"There was the corpse of a woman that died before dawn yesterday just some ten meters outside the main gate. I went there to take a walk before seeing the corpse. It was covered by ants and there was a bucket with some clothes in it next to her. I think those were the only belongings she had in this world. I asked a certain woman who sold cooked food in one of those sheds outside the hospital gate what happened. She told me that the woman arrived the previous day before she died looking very sick. She could not walk properly and was

213

also unable to talk. No one knew where she came from and what she was suffering from. She sat down at the spot her corpse was finally lying and someone gave her food to eat. She ate just a little and placed the rest next to where she sat. When I went there, her dead body was lying with her mouth in the plate of the leftover food. I guess it was the food that attracted the ants that covered her lifeless body. My friend, where is this world heading to? What has happened to our African values? Are we not supposed to be each other's keeper? How many doctors walked or drove in and out of that gate? How many nurses walked in and out of that gate? How many midwives walked in and out of that gate? How many Christians walked in and out of that gate? Can they say that they did not see that woman to give her assistance and that's why she finally died there unattended to? I guess there was nothing financial to benefit from the woman and she ended up like a rejected dog. We have allowed self interest and the love for money to erode our African values. Doctors and nurses seem to be interested only in the money they can extort from patients. Where are the good Samaritans?" he asked with a sigh.

"The last one left on board the morning train," I said. "If you keep asking those questions, you will end up with more questions in your hands than answers. All we can do is watch and pray."

We went to the maternity ward and found the baby asleep. His mother too was asleep. We did not want to disturb them and decided to go and sit on the bench that was outside the ward. We had not had time to say a word to each other when we heard some wailing coming from the direction of the casualty ward. It was obvious that someone had given up the ghost. I asked my friend if we could go there and take a closer look.

"There is no need to go there. It is clear that someone has died and it would not surprise me if the person has died with no nurse or doctor close by. It seems they are here to recover the money they used to bribe their ways into the different medical training schools. That is what corruption does….it kills more than a virus. After so much criticism from the international community the government has decided to do a few arrests. But the arrests seem to be very selective. For instance there was this secretary of state under the minister of secondary education. The woman is now in prison while her immediate boss, the minister of secondary education is a free man. That woman was arrested for embezzlement and the question we are asking is how she would have embezzled money without the knowledge of her boss. I don't really think that anything will ever change in this country," he said with yet another sigh.

"You seem to be seeing only darkness ahead. My friend, try to be positive sometimes. The government in place will not remain there forever. The state will remain but governments come and go. Things will change someday," I said.

"I like your optimism but would not like to see things the way you do. Did you listen to the 16:00 news on Radio Hot Cocoa?" he asked.

"No I didn't," I said.

"There was something really disheartening to hear," he began. "The mutiny at the Bamenda central prison was one of the items that spiced the news yesterday. According to the reporter who covered the story, a new prison boss was appointed some sixteen months ago. He happened to be a

Muslim from the northern part of the country and had his own ways of doing things. The first thing he did was to close the little chapel within the prison premises and asked the inmates to convert to Islam. They refused and in retaliation the prison boss stopped visitation rights from all pastors and other religious persons who formerly came there to give them spiritual and material assistance. A certain catholic priest who supplied medicines to the prison stopped visiting them because of harassments from the prison boss. At the moment the reporter was making his report, there was a corpse of an inmate who had been very sick for over a year and no one bothered to take him to the hospital. There was still another man there who was very sick and when interviewed about why he had not gone to the hospital, he said that the prison asked for a bribe of one hundred thousand francs before he could be allowed to go and receive treatment. Since he could not afford it, he was left there and now, he is probably waiting only for death. Another inmate who was interviewed testified that since the arrival of the new prison boss, seventeen inmates have died and the eighteenth was lying there that late afternoon yesterday. The reporter enumerated a number of problems the inmates faced there at the prison. He talked of one kind of food which they eat everyday and it is not well cooked or spiced, they sleep on bare floors and are not allowed to go for treatment unless they bribe those who can give them permission….the list is long," he said.

A brief moment of silence ensued during which my friend remained in a very pensive mood. I was so overwhelmed by the picture he painted that I did not know what to say. The extreme cruelty was what I could not really come to terms with. I could not imagine that someone would want to force people to change their faith and when they refused which is

216

their absolute right, they are left to die when they fall sick. Where was the freedom of worship which was well spelt out in the constitution? "Man's heart is desperately wicked," I said unconsciously.

"Indeed it is wicked my friend," Paul said. "Do you know what I make of it all? The mentality of that prison boss is a reflection of the way most people in positions of power in this country reason. They feel that prison is meant only for a certain category of people. That prison boss can afford to treat other people like animals or scum because he does not imagine himself one day being behind bars. They can do it now because it is their turn but there will come a time when the tables will turn."

There was a lot of emotion in his voice as he spoke and I could feel the anger in him. It was really painful for a human being to treat others like animals simply because they have been tagged criminals. That was not supposed to mean that those who were incarcerated had ceased to be human beings. As the saying goes 'All people whether free or imprisoned are criminals and those who are locked up are just unfortunate to have been caught'

"Do you know what announcement I heard on Radio Bamenda early this afternoon?" he went on. "It was announced that our Muslim prison boss has been relieved of his duties. In a state of law, he would not go away free. He would be arrested and tried and if found guilty, he would be locked up in that same prison for manslaughter. But that will not happen here. When those who come from the French speaking part of the country commit crimes here, they are immediately transferred over night. The authorities claim that the criminals are going to face the law but the truth is that once they are out of the borders of the English speaking zone, they are free men. Let our English speaking brother commit the same crime in the French speaking zone. He will face the full weight of the law. That prison boss comes from the French speaking zone and I'm sure he is already a free man. Why did I come back to this country?"

The conversation was too nerve wrecking and I wanted it to end. Besides, I did not know if his hatred for the system was turning into xenophobia for those on the French speaking side of the country. Though I could not blame him for feeling and thinking the way he did, nepotism was something I could not deny its existence. If people could get jobs mostly through connections, why could they not be protected when they commit crimes? I told my friend that I was going inside the ward to check on his wife and son. They were awake and she was trying to breastfeed him. Anything that touched the circumcised spot made the baby cry a lot. I felt really sorry for him. With the day almost over, I felt that it was time to go home and rest. We left the hospital at the same time and boarded separate taxis. He had to go home to leave the sheets that were dirty and to get clean ones and return to the hospital with, that same evening. As far as I was concerned, that was it for that day.

20

I did not go to the hospital to visit my friend and his family on the fourth day after his son was born. I only called him on his mobile to see how they were doing. I went on the fifth day instead because that was when they had to pack out of the hospital. I went and assisted in the packing of things and their transportation out of the hospital premises to a waiting taxi which we hired. We got to my friend's house at 13:20. His mother-in-law moved in from the village and was going to stay with them for the next two and a half to three months. She was supposed to assist her daughter in taking care of the baby during the day and at night. The only thing my friend's wife had to do was breastfeed the baby. She spent the rest of the time resting to regain her strength. I went and visited them on Sunday at home at 14:00 and met some guests who came to greet the new born baby. After their departure at about 15:50, everything on TV looked really boring. My friend's wife pleaded with me to tell them one of my dog stories as I promised the last time I narrated that of Coco to them. I had no problem with that especially as I knew it was going to make her happy.

"My next experience with dogs happened less than two years after the first one with Coco," I began. "It took place during the long vacation period when I travelled to Buea to spend the holiday with my uncle, Uncle Tom. He lived around Small Soppo neighbourhood. It was a neighbourhood inhabited mostly by rich people and most of the houses were fenced. Our house was on street one and situated on the left side on the way in. It was the second from the main road. The first house was inhabited by Cole Wilson, an American

Peace Corp volunteer. He had some two huge German shepherds and they were very wild. They guarded their master's house twenty four hours a day. Any visitor who wanted to visit Mr. Wilson had to either call him on his phone or call round when he or she was certain that he was at home. If the visitor was not certain and could not call, he or she had to come and peep from outside the gate at the main door into Mr. Wilson's house to see if it was open. Any stranger who came there in his absence and made the mistake of walking in through the gate had to spend the rest of the day there until Mr. Wilson returned. His dogs could only allow someone to get in but he or she could not get out if he or she was not accompanied by Mr. Wilson. All of us who lived around there knew that but it did not prevent me from falling into the hands of the dogs one day when Mr. Wilson was not in. What attracted me into Mr. Wilson's yard? There was a guava three that was in his yard and stood very close to the fence. Some of its branches extended and crossed over the fence. The guavas on the branches that extended over the fence had all been harvested and those that were on the branches within the fence were still much intact. To harvest those, one had to go in only when Mr. Wilson was around. So, on one fateful Thursday which was about a month after I got to Buea, my uncle left the house in the morning after giving me and my two cousins some work to do in his absence. It was to weed around the house and to empty the trash cans. By 11:20, we had finished everything and the only thing left to do was to play. We went out of our yard with our ball onto the road that led into the neighbourhood. There, we were joined by the kids of our neighbours. We played until it was almost 13:00 and we felt like eating something. Personally, I wanted to eat something but not cooked food.

What I really wanted was fruits and I think that craving was provoked by the guavas within Mr. Wilson's fence. My friends went to their houses and had their meals before coming back. I did not go to our house with my cousins though they called in vain for me to come and eat with them. I remained outside Mr. Wilson's fence wondering how I was going to get to the guavas within the fence without being troubled by the dogs. An idea came and it was to creep to the tree trunk using the branches that hung over the fence. I knew that guava trees were very strong and their branches could not break easily. For that reason I failed to examine my weight to see if the branch I was about to step on could bear it. As I stepped on it and was mid-way to the trunk, the extension over the fence left its place due to my weight. Of course it swung downward by way of gravity. I hung on it firmly to avoid not only a mighty fall but the dogs as well. Unfortunately for me, I was at a level where the dogs could just lift themselves up a little and get me. That was what one of them did by holding me by the shirt I wore and pulling me down completely. I thought they were going to eat me but they did not. What they did was that one came and laid on my left while the other laid on my right, thus blocking all escape routes. I tried everything humanly possible to get away from them but it seemed those dogs could read people's mind. There were some sticks under the guava tree where they held me and I thought of grabbing one and inflicting maximum pain on each of them. But each time I extended my hand to pick one, only the grumbling that they made caused me to withdraw. It was the same thing when I tried to pick stones that were just centimetres from me. Finding myself caught between the lion and the deep blue sea, I gave up trying to get away. At least there was one thing I could do and it was either to turn and lie on my back or on my stomach. But that was done under some strict supervision which was accompanied by some little grumbling perhaps to warn me not to try anything stupid.

My friends soon returned and could not find me. They got worried especially when my two cousins told them that I did not follow them to the house. They decided to call and behold I answered from within the fence. Some of them climbed on the fence and saw me lying between my two body guards. So, they embarked on a mission to free me. They went and got sticks, stones and any other weapons they could possibly find. They brought them and started a nonstop bombardment at the dogs. Do you think they ran away? They did not....they cried when the pains were unbearable and barked to scare off my friends but did not move an inch. Honestly I did not know what was wrong with those dogs. I think they were too obedient or rather took their job a little too seriously.

As for my friends, they soon gave up after discovering that no amount of missiles was going to force the dogs to let me go. They went and continued playing their football without me but came from time to time to check if I was ok. They did so by either climbing on the fence and peering under the guava tree or calling. When they called and I responded, they knew that all was fine and they went back to their game. Of course being a great lover of football, I got really furious at the dogs for keeping me under the guava tree against my will while my friends were enjoying themselves outside the fence. But there was nothing I could do.

At 17:00, Mr. Wilson opened his gate and walked. His eyes went first to his veranda and then to the direction of the guava tree. I imagined that since he did not see his dogs on his veranda, he knew that they must have been holding something hostage under the guava tree and so came to see who it was. He knew me very well and as soon as he saw me between the dogs, he exclaimed 'Oh my God' and quickened his steps to where I was. He drove the dogs away when he got to me and helped me to my feet.

"Have you been here long?" he asked.

"I am hungry," was my reply.

If I was hungry, it meant that I had been there for a long time and he understood. As he held me by my right hand and was taking me to his house, he turned back and looked at the pile of used arsenal. It was obvious that someone had tried to free me before failing. But it did not matter at that moment. He took me into his house and gave me some yam and ndole. I devoured it in a flash and told him that I wanted to go. He apologized for what his dogs did and saw me off at his gate. I ran back to my uncle's house before he returned. If he got home that day and learnt of what happened to me, I would have been in serious trouble. He had always warned us about venturing outside the gate but being kids, we always saw things differently. Thank God, he never learned about it. But just three days after that incident, my uncle took me to Bishop Rogan College to visit one of his friends who was a priest. When we were through, we got on a commercial motor bike to head back home. We passed through a neighbourhood which had many stray dogs and one of them started chasing us as we passed by. It almost bit my leg. What else on earth did I need to proof to me that dogs and I were meant to be only on parallel lines? The hand writing was clear on the wall and I couldn't just ignore it. I had to make a decision on that day and it was to always maintain a reasonable distance between myself and dogs. That's why whenever my friend asked me to accompany him anywhere I always asked if there were dogs there."

My friend's wife laughed with some tears spilling out of her eyes. Those around the table also laughed. That was what made me happy. I felt that I was useful as I put smiles on people's faces and laughter in their hearts. That made them in turn to always want to have me around. However, with my friend having enough company in his house, I felt that it was time to go and take care of my marriage business. I left them not long after eating and went back to my house. I met Helen there and she was there to take care of my food and put some order in and around the house. She left for their family house soon after. It was out of the question for her to sleep out of their house as it was already known around their neighbourhood that a suitor had already asked her hand in marriage. If she was to sleep out and the information spread, it was going to spice gossip around their neighbourhood. That was something to be avoided at all cost.

The next day which was Monday, my father came over from the village and we left for the Bamenda main market at 09:00. There we bought everything that was on the list given to us at the home of my father-in-law. We checked everything against the list when they were all assembled to make sure that nothing was lacking or in short quantity. Everything was just right and we took them home and waited for the next day to come.

The D-day finally came and my father, Uncle Joe, Paul and I left for the residence of my father-in-law. We arrived there at 09:05. All my father-in-law's relatives were already seated. Warm words of welcome came from every angle of the house as we entered. There were some reserved seats at one end of the house and we went and occupied them. We were given some time to settle down after which real business began. It was the father of Helen who spoke first and he began by welcoming us and thanking some of his family members who sacrificed their activities to be there. "That is a sign that you all love our daughter," he said.

After those warm words from my father-in-law, one of his sisters was asked to take the list which was handed to us a week earlier and check it against the items that we brought. She did and there was a round of applause when she confirmed that everything that was on the list was there. A woman getting involved in the checking of items was something new. That made me really proud to be associated with a family that was not resistant to change. In the past and in other cultures around the country, that would have been considered not only as an insult to men but an abomination. In Oshea village, women were still not allowed to eat eggs except when they were given permission by their husbands. Young men had to go through an initiation ceremony to be allowed to eat chicken. Anyone caught eating chicken without going through the initiation rite was summoned to the palace and fined. If the person caught was a woman, the punishment was more severe. Members of the village traditional council went to her residence and caught any animal or took any foodstuff that they could find. Many educated people in the city would call it primitivism and greed. I was glad that the woman was associated with the family of my in-laws but did not know of the realities back in their village.

After the checking was done, Helen was called out and she went to where her father stood. He had a traditional horn cup in his hand filled with palm wine. He took a sip from the horn cup and handed it to Helen.

"There is a young man here who has seen you as the most beautiful among all the women on this planet earth and has vowed that if it is not you, it will be no one else. Do you know him?" he asked.

"Yes father," she replied.

"Have you accepted him and are ready to be his wife?" he asked.

"Yes father," she replied.

"Did you make the choice out of your freewill or you have been pressured into accepting him?" he asked.

"He is my choice and I've made it out of my freewill," she said.

"In that case, I want you to take that palm wine to where the man you have chosen is sitting. Drink from that cup and hand it to him to drink as well and then bring back the cup to me," he said.

She brought it to where I was, took a sip and then knelt down before me before handing it to me. That was to be proof to everyone present that she was going to be a submissive wife. I took a sip and handed the horn cup back to her which she took to her father. More palm wine was poured into the horn cup as everyone in the house had to drink from it. That was to prove that they accepted our union and held no grudges against us. A clean handkerchief was brought out to accompany the horn cup as it went from mouth to mouth. That too was a new development and I understood why. The risks of mouth infections and personal hygiene made it imperative. But if that were to take place in a village setting, especially where elders who had never been to school were involved, they would have felt insulted. But the times were changing and even the staunch traditionalist in the most remote of villages had to, sooner or later, dance to the tune of modernity.

When the sipping was over, a meal was brought and everyone in the house had to eat it. That was equally to further cement the relationship between our two families. That too was soon over and the father of Helen called me and his daughter to where he stood. There, we went down on our knees and the whole house prayed over us. Helen and I moved to where I sat after that as husband and wife. The things I brought for her bride price were shared then and there. Every member of Helen's family got something and Helen's father said a few words before the rites ended.

"Anybody who has eaten anything in this house and has taken anything out of this house should only think good of these children we are uniting today. If you go to plot evil against them, it will turn against you. To our children and son-in-law, he can go ahead and organize their court and church weddings. Those ones are important but not more important to us than what has happened in this house today. We recognize this one more as marriage than those other ones," he said.

The real celebration started after that. The whole house was no longer obliged to eat a single meal but each and everyone had the choice to eat what he or she pleased. There was much to eat. From my estimation, my father-in-law spent more than twice what I and my family were asked to come along with as bride price. I think my father-in-law was marrying his daughter off just as the Europeans did. Many neighbours and friends joined the celebration and I was certain that it was going to spice conversations around the neighbourhood for the next few days. That notwithstanding, I expected the women there to come and take Helen away and then return to ask money for one reason or the other before bringing her back. That was the drama that formed part of most traditional wedding ceremonies around the country. But none of that happened that day. That too was a complete break from what obtained in the past. All in all, the ceremony was good and I was really impressed with the changes that were made from the very start. I left that day with my family members and friend and most importantly Helen at 16:05 for my house. A new beginning started for me and her. I prayed to God to give me the courage and perseverance to be able to sail through the permanent commitment I just made which more and more men tended to dread. Moreover, my uncle had some wise words for me as I went to see him off after he spent some time at my house.

"Son," he said. "In this life, you cannot afford to be happy without hurting someone though it might not be intentional."

"Uncle, I don't understand," I said.

"You have decided to marry Helen. Were there no other women that were interested in you? Helen too decided to stick to you. Were there no other men who were interested in her? Of course there were and she could not please all of them just as you could not please all the women who would have wanted to be in Helen's place. You had to make a choice and that choice was bound to make some people unhappy. That is the price we have to pay to be happy. Do you understand what I mean now?" he asked.

"Yes, I do," I replied.

"When we were at that ceremony, I was expecting either a young man or woman to walk in there to disrupt the occasion claiming that marrying the other person would be madness. Those kinds of things are very common these days. But the strange thing is that those who come disrupting on-going weddings claiming to be either Mr. or Mrs. Right and not the other person getting married soon abandon them whom they prevented from getting married in the first instance. What a strange world!!! But thank God, what I feared did not happen. For that reason, it is now left to you to make your marriage work because staying together is not easy. You now have to fight to proof to those people that you disappointed that you did not make a mistake. You know what they would say if things don't work out between both of you. I shall always be there to give a helping hand if you need one," he said.

I thanked him for his usual kind words and told him how lucky I was to have him. We parted when he boarded a taxi for his house.

21

The next day which was Wednesday, I got out of bed at 06:30 and called my friend. I asked him if it was possible for us to meet at the Bamenda III council. He told me he was going to be there before 08:00. I left the house at 07:20 and was there in 20 minutes. My friend was already outside the council premises waiting for me. As soon as I arrived we went into the council secretariat and a lady who sat behind a table requested to know what she could do for us. I told her that I wanted to legalize my union with my partner. Her eyes widened as the person next to me in front of her was not a woman but a man. She swallowed some spittle before asking her question. I guess she was scared of my reaction but the question had to be asked.

"Is your 'wife' the man next to you?" she asked.

Paul and I stared at each other before I answered her question.

"Oh no no no," I replied with a lot of insistence. "My wife is at home. We had our traditional wedding yesterday and she was feeling very tired today. I did not want to bother her and so decided to come with my friend. I have all her details with me," I said.

"That is very nice to hear. I must really appreciate your courage. Many people do not come for court weddings these days. You are the tenth person this year. Congratulations and I pray that heaven should grant your hearts' desires," she said.

We thanked her immensely and she went on to take out a receipt booklet from one of her drawers. She asked me to give her the sum of 5000 francs. I did and she issued a receipt with the amount written on it. She then asked me to come back there on Saturday with my partner and some two witnesses. With that information and receipt, we left the council premises.

Paul informed me of the arrival of his mother from the village the previous day shortly after he arrived home from my traditional wedding ceremony. I asked him how she was doing and he told me that she was not doing badly. I went on to ask him if he had, had a chat with her and what information she brought from the village. He sighed and shook his head. I knew there was something that was wasn't going right and asked him again what news his mother brought from the village.

"My elder brother has already sold a piece of land and used some of the money to bribe my uncles and other relatives to make him the successor," he said.

"Don't tell me that you had your eyes on the successor shit. You already have a house of your own and a family here in the city. Your preoccupation should be your family and not some thorny crown back in the village," I said.

"I am not interested in being my father's successor. What is annoying to me is the speed with which he sold the land. It seems he was just waiting for my father to die so that he could do what he wants. It would not surprise me if he confiscates everything and gives nothing to his other brothers and sisters. My mother told me that he had brought in a widow who is a mother of six and they have occupied the main house. He is spending part of the money from the sale of the land to take care of the woman's children in school while he has many and is not taking care of any of them. That is not the only aching thing; he asked my mother and my younger ones to move into the smaller house which is already collapsing. Can you believe that?" he asked.

232

"I would never have imagined that his greed would push him into doing such a thing even to his own mother. Some people can do really strange things. If that is the situation, it would be senseless going to repair the smaller house since you can't tell what he might decide to do one day. Your father left a lot of land and if I were you, I would go back there and establish a land certificate for one of the pieces of land. That would keep him off and you could then build a better house for your mother on it," I said.

"That was exactly what I thought of last night. Now that you have made the same suggestion, I am going to do just that. I have to do it fast because I don't want the old house collapsing on a family member. Besides, I don't want to keep my mother here for too long because she might soon fall out with my wife over I don't know what. My wife's mother is in my house to take care of her daughter and grandson. One can never tell what can spark between those two," he said.

I did not want to be in his place. My mother was already late and chances of my mother and Helen's mother ever clashing was impossible. One thing was clear and it was that wherever there was interest, there was bound to be clashes. People shall always be people and there shall always be interests to protect.

We soon boarded a taxi and I decided to go with my friend to the direction of his home. I wanted to say hello to his mother as well as see how the rest of his family were doing. We got outside his gate at 10:40 and walked into the yard. His mother was outside. She was drying her grandson's napkins. I greeted her and she was very happy to see me. She asked me why I hardly called her to say hello. I did not have an answer to her question but promised to start calling from then on. I then moved into the house with my friend to see how the baby and his mother were doing. They were all doing fine. I spent an hour with them before telling my friend that I had to go back home to start assembling material for the new academic year that was just a few days away. He went out with me to see me off. While we were outside his house, I asked him what he was going to do about his elder brother. His face turned dark as I mentioned his brother.

"That one is dead to me. It is obvious that he is going to squander everything my father laboured for because he does not know how to work for them. I'm sure he certainly went and told that widow of the property he had inherited from my father and she is there not because she loves him but because she wants him to take care of her children. When he wastes everything, she will probably take off with her children. I will not blame her for having that intention but my brother for being so stupid. He will start thinking straight again when everything is gone. That is when I will be his brother and cease to be a stranger. I swear that if he is dying and I'm the only one around him, I would watch him die," he said.

His last statement sent chilling waves down my spine and I told him what I made of it all.

"Do you sometimes listen to yourself speak? You really scare me sometimes with what comes out of your mouth. Did you just say those things out of anger or would you really do that if it happened?" I asked.

My friend remained silent.

"You are an educated man and I don't think you should be thinking of something like that. Rejection and hatred are all I could read in what you just said. Doing that would be going down to his level. You just have to be the good person you've always been and that would be a way of teaching your elder brother that those material things are not all that matter in life," I said.

It seemed my words of advice angered my friend further.

"What kind of lesson do you want my elder brother to read from my actions? He never reads and do you know why? It is because he thinks of nobody but himself. People like that should not be helped when they are in trouble," he said.

I decided to turn to the bible to calm him down.

"You are a Christian and you know what the bible says about loving your neighbours and enemies. Hating and rejecting your brother would be refusing to see God in him. You know that you will die someday and will want to go only to God. If that were to happen now, how would you want to go to Him whom you've already rejected in your brother? You can hate your brother's actions but do not hate him because you would hate God that lives in him as well," I said.

"You really know where to hammer to soften me," he said.

With those words coming from him, I jumped into a taxi and headed home.

Saturday did not delay in coming. The school reopening date was just five days from then. I left the house at 09:30 for the Bamenda III council with Paul and Jessica, Helen's friend. They were to be our witnesses at the signing of the marriage certificate. No family members accompanied us there because we told them that there was no need to. Instead, we asked everyone to wait for us at home where there was to be some feasting when we returned. However, when we got to the council hall, there was another couple already seated there with their witnesses. We went in and occupied our own seats. The mayor came in shortly after and gave some lectures before we went into the signing of papers.

"When I took over this office a few years ago, I organized my wedding and TV cameras were present. I wanted to live by example and encourage young men and women, even those that have been cohabitating for long to come forward and legalize their unions. Besides, it was not normal for me to legalize the unions of other people when mine was still pending. My actions encouraged a good number of people to come forward but the number has been dwindling over the years. Since this year started, I've not had up to twelve couples come forward. But I am not very disappointed. The fact that I have two couples in front of me today makes me happy. The fact that you are still very young makes me even happier. However, I see you in here looking very bright but are you going to stay together? Only time will tell the answer to that question. These days, people coming up to have a legal marriage are rare and the few that manage to come up, return shortly after asking for a divorce. It seems young people find it so hard living together these days. Parents seem to have taken up the cue and will soon over take the young people. It is now common to see women who tend to be single when they attain the age of 45 and above. What is happening? What can we do to stay together? First, we have to learn to be tolerant. If two brothers or two sisters from the same womb could fight, what more of two total strangers from different backgrounds and cultures? So, tolerance is the first thing. That happens to be the opposite of impatience and many young people seem to be suffering from it these days. The second thing is avoid as much as possible what your partner does not want. The third thing is to always be innovative. Always bring in something new to surprise your partner with. Marriage is a long term commitment and if it is subjected to routine for a long time, it would become boring.

The fear of being subjected to a boring routine is one of the reasons why young people are scared of getting married. So always try to spice your marriage with something new. The churches are now organizing something called Marriage Encounters. Those are places you should go and learn how you can make your marriage a better one. But even though I advise you to go to such encounters, they should not dictate the way you have to leave your lives. Basically, those are the three main ingredients you need to make your marriages work. On the other hand, one thing you must avoid is to stomach problems or use the teachings of the church to cover up what is hurting you inside. If your partner does something wrong, always create time to dialogue with each other. Accumulated unresolved problems soon develop into a time bomb and divorce is the ultimate outcome when it eventually explodes. We should try to avoid that. Let's therefore have the best interest of our partner at heart before initiating any action. The promises you make here today should be those you would keep. Pray to God to be your guide and helper," he said.

There were a lot of lessons in what he said and we were grateful for it. We proceeded to the taking of vows and the fitting of rings on our fingers. Next came the signings. There were three copies of the signed documents and a copy was given to us. We shared a crate of beer that we took there and handed the bottle of wine we bought to the Mayor. That ended the court wedding at the council premises and we headed for home.

We arrived home at 12:30 and our families were all there waiting for us. There were many people and our sitting room was far too small to contain everybody. For that reason, everything that had to be eaten and drunk and the chairs where people had to sit on were set outside on the yard under canopies. People were already feeling hungry and with the food already set, they were definitely not going to like speeches especially if they were lengthy ones. It was only my father who rose and thanked our families for coming together to celebrate the union of their children. He prayed to God to bless us with riches and children. He also prayed that God bless the food that was set on a large table in the yard. Everybody went to the table to get something to eat. Helen and I went into the house and changed into simple clothes and went out again. We went round serving our relatives and guests with food and drinks. We took the opportunity to thank those who came especially those that came from afar. The last people left our yard at 20:00. Tiredness set in and we went to bed.

The next day which was Sunday, we had a lot of work to do. We had to clean up the house and the plates that were used by our family members and guests. We were through at 13:30 and my attention shifted to the new academic year that was just a few days away. If there was any legacy I had to leave behind, it had to be connected to my teaching job. If I had to legalize things with Helen at the speed of light, it was because I did not want anything interfering with my job. Besides, I was going to be a father and was going send my child to school where I was going to expect those teaching him or her to put in their utmost best. It was therefore imperative that I put in my utmost best in the teaching of the children that were to be entrusted in my care.

Later that Sunday evening, Helen and I sat on the couch. She sat with her head on my lap. We talked of the future and the number of children we were going to have. She insisted on having three and I wanted just two. I was thinking of my

238

pocket before insisting on having just two. I did not know what she was thinking of. Death was something no one thought of especially when life was sweet but I felt that if death was to be unkind to one of us, the children should be manageable. There was no need having many children who would become burdens to other people. I hated thinking about that. We ended that day by planning to hold our church wedding in December. Later that evening, it was as though the world became a vast paradise and only the two of us inhabited it. Nothing else mattered and we wished everything to remain at a standstill. That was a wish provoked by the intense emotions of just one moment but the world had to continue turning.